ESCAPE
FROM THE CITY
OF THE DEAD

TALES FROM THE GOLDEN KINGDOM

ESCAPE FROM THE CITY OF THE DEAD

MARK ALLISON

The Book Guild Ltd

First published in Great Britain in 2021 by
The Book Guild Ltd
9 Priory Business Park
Wistow Road, Kibworth
Leicestershire, LE8 0RX
Freephone: 0800 999 2982
www.bookguild.co.uk
Email: info@bookguild.co.uk
Twitter: @bookguild

Typeset in 11pt Adobe Garamond Pro

Printed and bound by CPI Group (UK) Ltd, Croydon, CR0 4YY

ISBN 978 1913913 649

British Library Cataloguing in Publication Data.
A catalogue record for this book is available from the British Library.

To my two daughters, the real Hannah and Fleur, who
provided the inspiration behind this story.

1

BARNABY'S MILL

A bank of heavy grey cloud rolled slowly in from the north, blacking out the moon and stars and cloaking the world below in darkness. With the cloud came the rain. Gentle at first but soon torrential.

On a ridge, silhouetted against the dark sky, four cowled horsemen surveyed the narrow valley before them. It led first to an old water mill and then a school and a village of about two thousand souls. Two of the men turned and set off at a brisk canter towards the east. The other two urged their ponies forward and filed carefully along the narrow, rocky path which followed the stream down the valley.

All was silent at the mill. The only movement, that of the enormous wheel that turned the grindstone. The miller was at home, but the horsemen knew he'd long since gone to bed and wouldn't disturb them. They passed quietly and rode on down to the school. Surrounded by carefully manicured lawns, it comprised four buildings: the main school building, two blocks of classrooms and a refectory at the rear. The men dismounted, tethered their horses and made directly for one of the classrooms. They peered through the windows, as they'd done a hundred times before and, satisfied that everything was as it should be, they returned to their horses and retraced their steps back to the mill and up the valley to the ridge.

Their weeks of planning and preparation had been meticulous, and anything that could go wrong had been carefully considered. They were now ready to execute their plan. Their target was the school and tomorrow morning, as soon as the children arrived, they would strike.

As dawn approached the rain stopped, the clouds began to melt away and the horsemen turned away over the ridge. But as they did the fading moonlight briefly caught the sides of their faces and revealed something absolutely grotesque – something sinister and evil.

*

A little more than an hour's ride away, safe behind huge castle walls, a young girl and an ancient monkey lay fast asleep on a soft white bed in a big dark room. The girl was Princess Fleur, second daughter of the King and Queen of the Golden Kingdom. The monkey's name was Monkey and he'd been in the family so long that Lord Balthazar had once said he might be as old as the kingdom itself. That probably explained why he was completely threadbare and missing half a tail.

Outside the room a young woman tiptoed silently

down the long dark corridor and stopped outside Fleur's room. She pushed open the heavy double doors, stepped inside and turned up the bedside lamps. It was Hazel, Fleur's lady-in-waiting, come to wake her charge. She picked up Monkey, sat him down at the end of the bed with the rest of the soft toys, and gave Fleur a little kiss on the forehead and a gentle shake.

'Wake up, my little princess,' she whispered, 'it's time to get up.'

Fleur sighed and turned over.

'I don't want to,' she replied sleepily, 'it's too early and I'm still tired.'

'I think you've forgotten what day it is, haven't you?' Hazel said.

Fleur reluctantly stopped sucking her thumb for a moment and opened her eyes.

'What day is it?' she asked.

'Well, let's see,' Hazel said. 'For starters it's Midsummer's day which means it's fair day, for seconds you've got a fantastic class trip to Barnaby's Mill, and last, but not least, it's your birthday – you're seven today.'

That did the trick. Princess Fleur leapt up, flung her arms around Hazel's neck and jumped off the bed.

'What am I wearing?' she asked excitedly. 'Can I wear my new pink dress from Alcazar?'

'With all the chocolate you're going to be eating at Barnaby's Mill?' Hazel said. 'No, you certainly can't. I've laid out your dungarees, an old red T-shirt and pumps. You can wear the pink dress for your party this evening.'

Fleur was about to protest but she thought better of it. She knew Hazel was right: she'd be having mountains of chocolate and was bound to get it all over herself. So, she let out a pretend groan and ran off to her dressing room.

'I'm ready,' she said a few moments later, presenting herself to Hazel. 'Can I go now?'

'Have you washed you face, cleaned your teeth and brushed your hair?'

'Of course, I have,' Fleur said.

'Oh no you haven't, my girl,' Hazel replied. 'Now you get back in that dressing room and don't come out until you're spick and span.'

At last, Fleur was respectable enough to pass inspection, and with breakfast bag in hand, she gave Hazel a hug and a kiss and skipped off down the still dark corridor.

Down in the great hall things were already beginning to get chaotic. The boys were complaining noisily about having to be up so early, the girls were comparing outfits and poor Miss Preen, who looked as though she was still half asleep, was busily checking everyone off against her register. At last, cook arrived with bowls of steaming hot chocolate. That seemed to settle things down enough to allow Miss Preen to finish her checking and, as the sun began to rise, she led the children into the courtyard where two Royal carriages stood waiting. Each carriage was drawn by six magnificent white horses adorned with golden plumes. It took an age to get the children aboard. Despite Miss Preen's diligent checking, some had forgotten their snacks, others their school bags and some decided they needed to go to the loo once more. Eventually, though, when they'd all been counted on board for a final time, and the doors snapped shut, the coachmen flicked their whips, the horses lifted their proud heads and trotted out of the courtyard onto the long elegant boulevard that led to the castle's northern gate.

As they neared the gate, the coaches had to slow down. Despite the early hour people in great numbers were beginning to arrive for the fair. On the beautiful open lawns on either side of the boulevard, a market was already starting to spring up. Later on, it would be a hive of feverish activity as people from the castle sought out the finest fruit and freshest meat for their afternoon feast. In the evening, when the feasting was done, they would throng among the travelling musicians, poets, storytellers, jugglers, acrobats and magicians, and party until the early hours of the morning.

Eventually, the two coaches were through the castle gates, and the milling throng was behind them. They turned onto the Great North Road, and with another gentle flick of encouragement, the horses broke first into a brisk trot and then a steady canter.

The Golden Kingdom was at its beautiful best on Midsummer's day. The meadows on either side of the road were a magnificent carpet of emerald green and the orchards were bursting with ripening fruit. Wonderful juicy oranges, crisp red apples, the plumpest of delicious peaches, and field upon field of huge watermelons, grapes, strawberries, raspberries, blackberries and just about every other fruit you could think of.

After they'd been travelling for about an hour, there was a cry from the coachmen: 'Barnaby's Mill!' This was what the children had been waiting for and immediately they started climbing over each other and craning their heads out of the windows to have a look. The village was right ahead, nestled between two gently rolling hills and, just beyond it, where the valley began to narrow and rise, they could see the ancient mill. Soon they turned off the Great North Road and trotted along a pretty avenue lined with the cinnamon trees which flavoured the village's famous churros. They rolled into a lovely, wide cobbled square with a wonderful fountain in the middle. All around were cafes and restaurants, and, although it was still not even breakfast time, the waiters and waitresses were already setting out their tables and writing up their menus for the day's special holiday lunch. As the Royal coaches rolled bumpily across the square, everyone stopped to wave at them. They were especially eager to catch a glimpse of the Royal princess – Princess Fleur.

Leaving the square and the waving well-wishers behind them, the two coaches click-clacked their way up a long cobbled road which was bordered on both sides by more cinnamon trees. At the end was Barnaby's Mill School. It was a beautiful, ancient-looking school built of golden sandstone. There was a main building with a bell tower on top and, on either side, two smaller buildings that looked like classrooms. In front of the school there was a lush lawn around which the cobbled road divided before re-joining at the main entrance.

The children from year two (the same year as Fleur) were all waiting on the steps with their teacher. As their visitors approached they waved enthusiastically and, once the carriages had drawn to a halt, they helped everyone down and the teacher led them all to their classroom.

It was a large and cheerful room with beautiful oak-panelled walls and tall open windows which let in lots of light and fresh air. As was the custom throughout the Golden Kingdom, the schoolroom was built on two levels. At the front of the class a dais ran from wall to wall. This was the teacher's domain, a vantage point from which she could survey her charges and throw pieces of chalk at any whisperers or daydreamers. In the middle stood her grand table, flanked on either side by two huge blackboards. Below the dais, there were four rows of neatly spaced two-seater desks. Each had a sloping top and an attached wooden bench. Along the top edge were two inkwells and a long, narrow groove for pens and pencils.

The Barnaby's Mill children had been instructed to mingle with their guests and get to know them as soon as they arrived so, as they entered the classroom, they each took a visitor by the hand and led them to a desk. Princess Fleur's hand was grabbed by a cheeky-looking girl with short fair hair, big blue eyes and sticky fingers. She hurried Fleur to the back of the room and sat her down as far away from the teacher as it was possible to get.

'Hello,' she said with a mischievous grin, 'I'm Esme.'

'And my name's Fleur.'

'I know it is,' Esme said, 'you're Princess Fleur.'

As soon as the children were sat at their desks, the teacher stepped onto her dais. That was the signal for silence, known to every child in the kingdom and, immediately, quiet descended on the class.

'I'm Mrs Pole,' she began, with a soft voice and warm smile. 'I'm the Class Two teacher here at Barnaby's Mill School, and on behalf of the class, the school and the whole village I'd like to extend the warmest of welcomes to our visitors.'

On that note, Princess Fleur jumped to her feet.

'And on behalf of our class, Mrs Pole, and our school, and the entire palace, I would like to say how grateful we are for your invitation and how happy we are to be with you today.'

'Thank you very much,' said Mrs Pole. 'Now, if I may, I'd like to explain what we've got lined up for you today. First Master Kernel, our head miller, and Master Ball, our chocolate expert, are going to introduce themselves. Then Master Kernel, or Windy, as he prefers to be called, is going to take you to the mill to grind some wheat and show you how to make churros. When you get back I'm going to tell you a little bit about the history of Barnaby's Mill: about the man called Barnaby who built the first mill all those years ago, and about his grandson who planted the first chocolate tree. I'm going to explain how the village has grown from such humble beginnings into the famous producer of delicious churros and fine chocolate it is today. After that, we'll have a short break and then Master Ball, who teaches Class Six and, as I've just said, is one of the kingdom's leading experts on chocolate, is going to explain exactly how chocolate is grown and how different parts of the kingdom specialise in different types of chocolate. Did you know, for example, that some places, like Barnaby's Mill, specialise in growing Canopy Chocolate? That's the dark chocolate which grows above the canopy, while others specialise in Under-leaf Chocolate, the lighter brown chocolate which hangs and matures below the canopy, and others still specialise in the mysterious art of growing Ground, or Dappled, Chocolate. And when Master Ball has finished in the classroom I believe he's going to take

8

you to one of the groves to pick a few bunches of our finest Canopy Chocolate for yourselves.'

'Excuse me, Miss, may I ask a question?' said one of the boys from Princess Fleur's class.

'Certainly,' Mrs Pole replied, 'and your name is?'

'Fredegar, Miss, Master Fredegar.'

'We call him Freddy,' Princess Fleur whispered to Esme. 'He's a bit weird, he's always asking questions.'

'Well, Master Fredegar,' Miss Pole continued, 'what's your question?'

'I heard my father say that in some parts of the world chocolate doesn't grow on trees the way it does here in the Golden Kingdom. Instead, it's made by roasting and grinding little beans and then mixing the powder into a kind of hard paste. Have you ever heard that story, Miss? Do you think it's true?'

'I've certainly heard the story,' Mrs Pole replied, 'but I'm not sure how true it can be. It sounds to me as though chocolate made that way would be horribly gritty. On the other hand, who knows what happens in lands beyond the Golden Kingdom? I suggest it would be a good question to put to Master Ball. If anyone knows the answer it's sure to be him.

'Now,' she continued, 'after your visit to the chocolate grove the plan is to come back here and have some hot chocolate and churros before the coaches come to take you back to the castle. So, I think now's a good time to share some exciting news with you. I'm happy to tell you that, apart from being Midsummer's day, today is very special for another reason. It's Princess Fleur's seventh birthday and she's kindly invited everyone, her own class and ours, to a party at the palace this evening. Parents have been informed and you'll be relieved to know they've all agreed. Everyone will spend the night at the palace and return home tomorrow morning. So, assuming you all think it's a great idea, I suggest we have a big round of applause for Princess Fleur.'

The whole class leapt to their feet and clapped and cheered as loudly as they could. Once the excitement and applause had subsided, Mrs Pole spoke again.

'As you can see, children, we've got a very busy day ahead of us, so I suggest we fortify ourselves with breakfast. Normally we take our meals in the refectory but since today's Midsummer's day and everyone's on holiday, including cook, we're going to have it here in the classroom. There's a huge urn of hot chocolate on the table over there by the window, and under that white cloth is a mountain of delicious cinnamon-coated churros. Masters Kernel and Ball will be here soon, so I suggest you tuck in straight away.'

On that note, the boys leapt to their feet and charged over to the breakfast table, attacking it like a pack of starving wolves. So savage was the frenzy that Mrs Pole had to call them to order and remind them to leave something for the girls.

'This is the best hot chocolate I've ever tasted,' Princess Fleur said to Esme and the other girls who'd all crowded round their table.

'It can't be as good as the chocolate you get in the palace,' Esme said. 'Surely that must be the best in the whole kingdom.'

'It's certainly very good,' Princess Fleur replied, 'but I think this is the best I've had.'

'Princess Fleur,' Esme continued, 'none of us Barnaby's

Mill girls have ever met a real-life princess before, so do you think you could tell us a little about what it's like being a princess and living in a palace?'

'On one condition,' Princess Fleur replied, with a smile on her face. 'You must call me Fleur and not Princess Fleur. Now then, what would you like to know?'

'What's the palace school like?' asked a little red-headed girl called Jemima. 'Is it true that you learn about magic and mysteries and fabulous lands, and that your teachers are princesses from foreign kingdoms?'

'Well, I don't know who told you that,' Fleur replied, laughing. 'It's nothing like that. In year two, all our lessons are really boring. We have Reading, Writing and Numbers every single day, and on Mondays, Wednesdays and Fridays we have double Morals and Manners, which is about the most boring lesson ever invented.'

'So, nothing about magic or fabulous lands?' Esme asked, obviously surprised and a little disappointed.

'Nothing at all. My sister told me that in year seven we'll do three new subjects: People and Places, Myths and Magic, and Alchemy and the Great Mysteries, but she said the teachers even manage to make those subjects boring.'

'So, your teachers aren't princesses from foreign lands?'

'No, our teacher's called Miss Preen. She's very nice and very kind, but I don't think she's ever been out of the Golden Kingdom, and she's certainly not a princess. Anyway, you'll see her for yourselves this evening. She's sure to be at the party.'

'What's it like having a king for a father?' asked Rufus, one of the boys.

'I've never had any other kind of father,' Fleur replied.

'So, I don't know what other ones are like. My father's very busy all the time so I don't see much of him during the day. But he nearly always tells me my bedtime story.'

'What kind of stories does he tell?' Robin, one of the other boys, asked. 'He must know millions of tales about famous knights and battles, and dragons and trolls.'

'He does,' Fleur replied. 'Every story is different and they're always exciting. He's better at telling stories than either my mother or Hazel.'

'Who's Hazel?' Esme asked.

'She's my lady-in-waiting,' Fleur replied. 'Her stories are good, but they're not as good as my father's.'

'Tell us about Sir Alfred,' another boy called Will said. 'Is it true that he's looking for a troll to fight?'

'I'm not sure,' Fleur replied. 'I know he's already killed a dragon and a witch and that killing a troll would make him a three-star knight, but I don't think he spends all his time looking for trolls.'

'But it would make him the most famous knight in living memory,' Will went on. 'The last three-star knight was Geoffrey the Dragon Slayer, and he lived centuries ago.'

'Maybe it would,' Fleur replied, 'but I think he's going to marry my sister.'

'What a waste,' Will said. 'Is Sir Alfred going to be at the party this evening?'

'I think so. So, you can ask him then.'

'I've got another question,' Esme said. 'Is it true that Lord Balthazar has a huge telescope at the top of the castle's highest tower, and that he uses it to watch out for badly behaved children?'

'It's true that he has a telescope at the top of the Great Tower, but I'm sure he doesn't use it to spy on naughty children. He's much too busy for that. Whenever I've seen him at his telescope he's always looking at the stars. It looks really boring to me, but he seems to like it, and he's always writing notes about what he sees.'

'I told you,' Jemima said to Esme. 'It's just what parents say to stop children from talking and messing about at bedtime.'

'Can I ask you a question, Fleur?' a rather shy-looking girl called Rosie asked.

'Of course you can,' Fleur replied, 'what is it?'

'What are you going to wear for your party this evening?'

'I've got a brand-new dress from Alcazar. I've never worn it before so I'm going to wear that.'

'Wow!' Jemima said. 'Is it really from Alcazar?'

'It is,' Fleur replied.

'And what's it like?'

'It's lovely. It's got lots of little fauns embroidered on it.'

'And is it magical?' Esme asked. 'We've heard that all the dresses from Alcazar are enchanted.'

'Not all of them,' Fleur replied. 'But this one is. It was made by Sabrina, who's a direct descendant of Zina, the very first dressmaker to make magical dresses.'

'And how's it enchanted?' Jemima asked. 'What does it do?'

'When I'm standing still it doesn't do anything. It's just like a normal dress. But when I start to twirl round or dance it comes alive and the fauns dance with me.'

'So, the legend's true then? There really was a dressmaker and a djinn?'

'Of course it is,' Fleur replied. 'And I've got other enchanted dresses. I'll show you them tonight. You can all have a twirl in them, if you like.'

'Have you actually been to Alcazar?' asked Will, whose ears had suddenly pricked up. 'What's it like?'

But before Fleur could answer, Fredegar jumped in.

'I can tell you what it's like,' he shouted excitedly. 'It's a desert kingdom called the Jewel of the Sands. It's the Golden Kingdom's oldest ally, and one of the most famous places in the world. My father's been there lots of times and he's told me all about its silver domes, luxurious gardens and the Silver Riders.'

'Who are they?' Will asked.

'You mean you've never heard of the Silver Riders?' Fredegar said, with a tone of mock astonishment. 'They're the most famous knights in the world, after the Golden Companions.'

'He's off again,' Princess Fleur whispered to the girls. 'According to Freddy, his father's been all over the world and seen just about everything there is to see.'

It seemed that there was no end to the children's questions or to Princess Fleur's willingness to happily paint for them a picture of what it was like to be a Royal Princess. But before she or her classmates from the palace could start asking their questions about life at Barnaby's Mill, the hot chocolate and churros had all disappeared, and Mrs Pole stepped onto the dais.

'Now, children, there will be plenty of time for lots more chitchat later on, but for now I'd like you to return to your desks and welcome Masters Kernel and Ball.'

As before, the lively chatter ended immediately, and

silence descended on the class once more. The door opened and in strode the two men. They couldn't have been more different. Master Kernel was tall and craggy with a tanned, weather-beaten face and white powder in his wild grey hair. It was clear to anyone that he must spend most of his time working outside in the sun, or in his dusty old mill. His shirt was unbuttoned nearly to his waist and his sleeves were rolled up to his elbows. Master Ball, on the other hand, couldn't have been more aptly named. Everything about him was round. He had a huge round stomach, a shiny round bald head and huge round eyes that were magnified to even greater hugeness by a pair of round spectacles which rested on top of his tiny round nose.

'No guesses who's who,' Esme whispered to Princess Fleur, with a cheeky laugh. 'We call him Master Pea because everything about him is like a pea.'

'Isn't that a little cruel?' Princess Fleur asked with a sympathetic frown. 'He probably can't help being that shape and he's got a very kind-looking face.'

'No,' Esme replied, 'it's just a bit of fun. We love him really, he's kind and he's a very good teacher but, you can't deny it, he does look like a pea. He knows we call him Master Pea and he doesn't mind a bit. He says it's because of his job. Being a chocolate expert means that he has to travel all over the Golden Kingdom, testing and judging chocolate. He says that he eats so much that it's hardly surprising he looks like one of the fattest of his canopy berries.'

Master Ball stepped forward to the edge of the dais and was just about to address the class when, without warning, the classroom door burst open and in charged four desperate-looking creatures whirling heavy wooden clubs about their heads. The first rushed at Master Ball and smashed him in the face with his club, shattering his glasses and sending him crashing to the floor in a pool of blood. The second attacked Master Kernel in the same savage way. A flashing club burst the miller's nose and sent a spray of blood all over Mrs Pole. Then, the other two turned to Mrs Pole and the children.

2

THE KING'S COUNCIL

On Midsummer's day, the King's Council chamber would normally be empty. Today, however, all but five of the seats at the great round table were occupied. It was the twelve Elders: distinguished lords and ladies of the Golden Kingdom who made up the Council and whose elevation to such a lofty and responsible position was a reflection of duties performed and abilities proven over many years. Their job was to discuss affairs of state and provide the King and his First Minister with sage advice. Around them was a circle of desks and tables occupied by a supporting team of secretaries and scribes.

They had no idea why they'd been called away from their families and friends on this of all days. Never in living memory had it happened before. However, they knew the decision to do so would not have been taken lightly, and they assumed that something of the greatest importance had happened. As they awaited the arrival of the King they sat in silence, looking first at the great doors at the end of the chamber and then at the man standing at the window.

It was he who had summoned them. He was Lord Balthazar, the King's First Minister. He was a strange-looking man: as tall as a tree and thin as a reed. His face looked as ancient as the world itself, but in that face shone the brightest eyes you ever saw. His knowledge and learning were unmatched, and his powers as magician and physician were legendary. He wasn't only the most powerful man in the land after the King; he was, without doubt, the wisest.

Suddenly the wait was over and the silence broken. The doors were flung open and the King swept into the chamber followed by the Queen, Princess Hannah, his daughter, and her husband-to-be, the renowned knight, Sir Alfred.

'My Lord,' said the King, striding towards Lord Balthazar. 'What on earth has happened to warrant this? Why have all these good people been torn away from their families and festivities on Midsummer's day? Has something terrible befallen us?'

Lord Balthazar showed the King and Sir Alfred to their places at the round table and courteously helped the Queen and Princess Hannah into theirs. He sat in his own place directly facing the King.

'I am afraid it has, My Lord. I bear the very worst news imaginable. Our little princess, Princess Fleur, has been taken.'

'Taken? What do you mean, taken?' the King demanded. 'Who's taken her? And where?'

'At this point, My Lord,' replied Lord Balthazar, 'we don't know.'

'And what have they taken her for?' the Queen asked.

'Again, My Lady, I fear I'm unable to give you an answer.'

'Then what do you know?' the King asked with a ring of impatience in his voice.

'Your Majesty,' Lord Balthazar said calmly, 'with your permission I will recount the events of the day and explain the little we *do* know.'

The King waved his approval, exchanged a worried glance with the Queen and sat forward in his chair. Silence fell upon the chamber once more, and all eyes fixed upon Lord Balthazar.

'Your Majesties,' he began, looking directly at the King and Queen, 'events unfolded as follows: As you know, Princess Fleur joined her class this morning on a year-two visit to Barnaby's Mill. It's an event that has taken place on Midsummer's day for as long as I can remember. I'm led to understand that the journey there was uneventful and the carriages arrived before breakfast, as planned. The children were welcomed, given breakfast and the year-two teacher, Mrs Pole, explained the agenda for the day. After she'd introduced the two men who were going to assist in the day's instruction, the miller and head chocolatier, four creatures burst into the classroom. They disabled the two men and dragged Princess Fleur from her desk. They thrust a rough potato sack over her head and tied it with a cord around her waist. One slung the sack over his shoulder and, followed by another, marched out of the room. The two creatures that remained drove Mrs Pole and the children into a corner of the room, leaving the miller and the chocolatier bleeding on the floor.'

The room was stunned by these words.

'You say these events happened at breakfast?' the King asked.

'That is so,' Lord Balthazar replied.

'Then why has it taken so long to summon this meeting and inform us? It's hours since this happened; evening is almost upon us.'

'My Lord, the two creatures that remained in the classroom kept everyone prisoner.'

'And you're saying that during the course of the entire day there were no visitors or passers-by? No-one to raise the alarm?'

'Unfortunately, that is correct, My Lord. The whole of Barnaby's Mill was in the village square enjoying their Midsummer's feast and festivities. No-one would have felt any need to check that the children were alright. They were in the excellent and experienced hands of their teacher, Mrs Pole, and two other responsible people, the miller and the chocolatier. We must remember that nothing like this has ever happened before. As far as I understand, no-one noticed anything suspicious in the days leading up to Midsummer's day. There were no strangers about. There was absolutely no warning.'

'So, when exactly was the alarm raised?' the King asked.

'When the two palace coaches returned to collect the children. The moment they arrived, the two remaining creatures left the classroom and fled the scene on horseback.'

'Who are these monsters? Do we know anything about them?' the Queen asked, utterly horrified.

'We have a very good description, My Lady. Miss Pole and the children had the best part of a day to observe them. It appears that they're men, or at least man-like. They're tall and muscular with dark reddish skin. Apart from a short, leather skirt around the waist, and leather leggings, they were naked. Their heads were shaven except for a knot of black hair gathered in a thick band at the back of the head. One wore his hair in a long pony-tail; the other had it in a braid. I'm told that their entire heads and cheeks were covered in ornate grey-blue tattoos which formed strange geometric patterns. But strangest of all were their faces. It seems that they practise facial mutilation. Their noses had been removed, leaving two open slits, their ears had been clipped into points, and their upper lips had been completely cut away to reveal teeth which had been painted red and filed to a sharp point. Mrs Pole said the mutilation contorted their faces into a permanent, malevolent grin.'

'May the heavens preserve us,' the Queen said.

'Could those poor children provide any further information?' the King asked.

'A little, My Lord. For the most part, the afternoon was spent in silence but there were a few occasions on which the creatures spoke to each other. The children said their speech was a snake-like hissing snarl, punctuated with a great deal of spitting and grinding of teeth.'

'And these dreadful beasts have taken my darling Fleur,' the Queen said, at last breaking down into a flood of tears.

Princess Hannah took her mother into her arms to try and offer some small comfort, but she too was overcome with horror. In fact, the whole chamber was in a state of shock. Lord Balthazar's words appeared to have frozen the secretaries and scribes whose job it was to note proceedings, while the elders looked at him in disbelief. Half of them had broken into tears. Even the King looked as though he'd been hit by a thunderbolt. There were no tears, but the colour had completely drained from his cheeks. He looked a very worried man.

'Have you ever encountered these creatures before, or heard of them?' he asked.

'No,' replied Lord Balthazar. 'If I had, I would not have forgotten them. I have neither heard people speak of them on my travels, nor come across any reference to them in my readings. Have any of you elders heard of them before?' he asked, looking round the table.

As one, they shook their heads in silence. This was the first anyone in the chamber had heard of these creatures.

'Do we know where they might have taken my sister?' Princess Hannah asked, between sobs.

'No-one actually saw their departure from the school, My Lady, but Mrs Pole feels sure they galloped off towards the north, and that was certainly the route taken by their accomplices this afternoon.'

'Is anyone pursuing them, My Lord?' Sir Alfred asked.

'Yes, Sir Alfred, let me explain the steps I've taken so far. As soon as the news reached me, I took two courses of action. First, I summoned the hound, appraised him of the situation and sent him off in immediate pursuit. The two creatures that fled when the coaches arrived have an hour's lead on him, perhaps an hour and a half, but I believe he'll catch up with them. His instructions are to determine where the other two are headed, the two that took Princess Fleur this morning.'

'Excuse me, My Lord, but who or what is the hound?' The Queen asked.

'Forgive me, My Lady, it's Sir Harry, one of Sir Alfred's fellow knights and our most accomplished ranger and tracker. If anyone can pick up the trail and get to these demons it is he. I've also instructed him to find out whatever he can from any villages they passed through, and to send riders back to me with regular updates.'

'My Lord,' Sir Alfred said, 'you described these creatures as being big and muscular, and we know from their actions that they're no strangers to savagery. Doesn't that put Sir Harry in danger? Wouldn't it make sense for me to set off after him to even the odds a little?'

'No,' replied Lord Balthazar, 'I understand any knight's first instinct must be pursuit and I'm sure we all appreciate the offer. However, I must decline. I'm aware that I've put Sir Harry in danger but I'm confident he has both the skills and experience to complete his task. Let us not get carried away by what we've heard of these creatures. They've succeeded in subduing three elderly adults and a class of seven-year olds. I'm not sure they'll find things so easy against a battle-hardened warrior, let alone a knight of the Golden Companions. Besides, Sir Alfred, I may well have other tasks for you.'

'You said you'd taken two courses of action, My Lord,' Sir Alfred continued.

'The second course of action was altogether broader in its scale. Immediately after sending Sir Harry on his mission I despatched Grey Falcons to the lords of the Four Towers.'

As everyone in the Golden Kingdom knew, the Grey Falcon was the fastest bird in the world after the golden swift. But while the golden swift can fly at top speed for only a few moments, the Grey Falcon can sustain high speeds over long distances. For example, they can fly from the Golden Castle to each of the four corners of the kingdom in a day, and for that reason, they are used to carry messages to and from the lords of the Four Towers. In flight, they are almost invisible. From below their feathers take on the colour of the sky, and from above, that of the land. They are the chameleons of the sky. Their native land is the foothills of the Flaming Mountains beyond the Great East River, but a number of breeding pairs have long been kept in the Golden Kingdom. Apart from the King and the lords of the Four Towers, the only other person allowed to keep them is the Captain of the Guard at King's Crossing. There is, of course, a colony at Alcazar (where they are known as the Veiled Falcon), which enabled speedy correspondence between the two kingdoms.

Lord Balthazar continued. 'The falcons carry instructions to initiate operation dragnet with immediate effect.'

'What's operation dragnet?' Sir Alfred asked, surprised that as a knight of the Companions and son of Lord Lupus, he'd never heard of it before.

'Operation dragnet is a special military operation that was perfected many years ago. Its purpose is to seal the borders of the Golden Kingdom and to assist in the apprehension of any unwelcome guests who may be abroad in our lands and bent on doing us harm. As soon as your father, Lord Lupus, receives his instruction he will divide his forces into two columns. One column will be sent east following the foothills of the Snowy Mountains; the other will march south along the banks of the Great West River. Lord Aguila will do the same. Operating from his castle, the Eagle's Nest, in the north-east corner of the kingdom, he will send one force west along the margin of the Snowy Mountains to join up with Lord Lupus's men. The other force will move south along the banks of the Great East River. Lords Drago in the south-east and Orcus in the south-west will despatch their forces in the same way until the entire kingdom is encompassed by a ring of steel. At that point, we will start drawing in the net until it reaches the Golden Castle. Our hope and expectation is that nothing will escape. These dreadful creatures will be snared like helpless rabbits and Princess Fleur brought back to us.'

'When do you expect the falcons to reach their destination?' the King asked.

'I despatched them within half an hour of hearing the news,' Lord Balthazar replied. 'They should be with the four lords late tomorrow afternoon.'

'Will that give the lords enough time to close the net before these creatures reach the border?' the King asked.

'It should do, My Lord. Even if the creatures travel without rest, it's unlikely they could reach the nearest border in less than four days. We should be able to close the net within three days, which means we'll have the best part of a day to spare. And if the creatures take any rest we'll have even longer.'

'If they *were* to cross the border before we manage to close the net, do we have any idea at all where they could be heading?' the King asked.

'No,' replied Lord Balthazar. 'Assuming they continue in a northerly direction there are, I think, three possibilities. They could make for the Snowy Mountains and one of the passes to the lands beyond. That would be the most direct route out of the kingdom. Alternatively, they could turn north-west and make for The Stones to cross the Great West River. That would take them into the Emerald Forest and the ocean beyond. Thirdly, they could turn east and head for the Ring of Fire or the Great East River.'

'How confident can we be that they'll continue north?' Sir Alfred asked. 'They may well have changed direction soon after leaving Barnaby's Mill.'

'They may have,' Lord Balthazar replied. 'We can't be sure of anything, but operation dragnet means we should be able to cut off any escape route. We should have a clearer picture of their true direction in a few hours, when riders start coming in with updates from Sir Harry.'

'Have you any idea who could be behind this?' Sir Alfred asked. 'Is there any chance that Blacknail could be involved?

'Absinthia Blacknail?' the Queen cried, nearly falling off her chair, clearly horrified by the suggestion. 'I thought that witch was dead. I thought you'd killed her, Sir Alfred.'

'We have never been sure of that, My Lady,' Lord Balthazar replied. 'As you well know, a combination of sword and spell reduced her to a badly damaged toad, but despite her injuries she was able to drag herself away and Sir Alfred, weakened by his own dreadful injuries, was unable to follow and finish her off. He did not actually witness her death that day.'

'So, she's still alive. Is that what you're saying?' the Queen asked.

'No, My Lady, I'm saying we can't be certain she died that day. Her injuries were severe and it's very likely that, even if she survived the weasels and stoats that prey on toads in those woods, she would succumb to them in time. On the other hand, we must not forget that, over many years, she's demonstrated remarkable resilience and a will to survive. The simple truth is we just don't know.'

'But even if she did survive, what evidence do we have of any link between her and these creatures?' the King asked.

'None whatsoever, My Lord,' replied Lord Balthazar. 'We can speculate as much as we want, but the fact is, at the moment, we just don't have enough information to construct any viable theories. My recommendation is that Princess Fleur will best be helped if we focus on gathering as much information as we can, rather than indulging in idle speculation.'

'And how do you propose to do that, My Lord?' the King asked.

'I expect that Sir Harry will soon be able to provide some facts. On top of that I propose two immediate courses of action. First, I'm asking the professors of the academy and you, the elders, to scour every nook and cranny in the library and castle archives, and to search every book, scroll, ancient parchment or map that might provide a clue, anything at all, as to who these creatures are.'

Lord Balthazar then turned to the scribes and secretaries who, since recovering from their shock, had been busily recording everything that had been said.

'Master Melchior,' he said, 'I'd like you to put together a team to explore the catacombs.'

'As you command, My Lord,' his secretary replied, 'but as you know, the catacombs are currently sealed.'

'I know. As soon as we're finished here I'd like you and your team to come to my office. The catacombs are labyrinthine and dangerous, and you will need clear instruction. Once everyone understands their task I will remove the seal.

'Now, with your permission, Your Majesty,' Lord Balthazar continued, 'I'd like to bring this meeting to an end. There is much to do, and time is of the essence.'

3

THE ROAD TO NOWHERE

Sir Harry picked up the trail soon after arriving at Barnaby's Mill. He had chosen one of the most powerful stallions in the castle stables and was confident he could run his prey down before nightfall. Once that task was accomplished he would push on through the night in pursuit of his real prey, the two demons that had abducted Princess Fleur.

The late afternoon light was good, and his practised eye easily identified tracks made by five horses. The fact that it was Midsummer's day made his task easier. Most people stayed at home so there were very few other tracks to cover those of his prey. After galloping hard for around an hour, the first village, Hare's Heath, came into view. Unlike Barnaby's Mill, which lay some way off the main road, Hare's Heath straddled it. Anyone travelling the Great North Road would have to pass straight through the village. On Midsummer's day it was sure to be crowded and no-one would pass unnoticed, so Sir Harry expected the tracks to leave the road and make a detour around the village to avoid attention. He reigned in his horse and continued at a trot, carefully studying the tracks. Sure enough, just before the village, they turned off the road and headed onto the heathland. A less experienced tracker would probably have lost them in the heather and grass, but Sir Harry had no such difficulty and, as he expected, they re-joined the road once the village was well behind. Secure in the knowledge that he was still on their trail, he turned back and cantered into the village square to see if anyone had seen anything.

The arrival of a knight in the village was always a cause for excitement. The arrival of so well-known and highly regarded a knight as Sir Harry, on Midsummer's day, was doubly exciting, especially for the children, and before he'd even had time to jump down from his horse, a waving and cheering crowd had begun to gather around him. Just as he thought he was about to be swept away by a joyous tide of welcome, a thunderous voice stemmed the flow.

'Make way, make way. Give the noble knight some room, if you please.'

A huge bear of a man with flowing black hair, a long bushy beard and a beaming smile pushed his way through the crowd. Unmistakably, it was Sir Brian, the larger-than-life village elder. Years ago he'd been one of the most famous knights in the land and had ridden with the King on many adventures, but eventually time had caught up with him, his joints had stiffened and with great regret he had laid down his arms. Many ageing knights feel so committed to their calling that they're unable to give up the service completely. They retire to one of the Four Towers where they see out their days training and mentoring young novice knights. Not so for Sir Brian. He made a complete break. He retired from the Knighthood and returned to Hare's Heath, the village of his boyhood, where, after a number of years of dedicated and distinguished service, he was elected village elder, and a very popular one at that. The custom in the Golden Kingdom was that elders were always addressed as Master or Mistress, but Sir Brian always insisted on 'Sir' in recognition of his time in the Knighthood.

'Sir Harry, Sir Harry,' he bellowed, thrusting out a hand, 'what a welcome surprise. Are you come to dine with us a while? Quickly, my friends, make room for our noble knight. Some meat and wine, if you please.'

'No, no, my friend,' Sir Harry replied as this bear of a man ushered him to his table where a place was quickly being set. 'Regrettably, I must decline your kind offer. I can't stay. I'm on the King's business.'

'The King's business, on Midsummer's day? It must be urgent.'

'Indeed it is, Sir Brian. Is there somewhere quiet we can talk?'

'Certainly, my friend, come to my office,' and he showed Sir Harry across the square to his office in the village hall, where they were quickly joined by the other members of the council.

Sir Brian and the councillors listened with mounting horror as Sir Harry recounted the terrible events of the day. Such dreadful news as this was too much for Sir Brian. As a former companion of the King, he had always been a regular visitor to the palace, and he felt great affection for both Royal princesses. He leapt to his feet, crashed his giant fist on the table, and thundered a long resounding, 'Nooooooo!' which almost shook the building, before bursting into a torrent of heart-felt tears. Anyone who didn't know Sir Brian, would have been amazed to see such an enormous mountain of a man reduced to tears in this way, but his friends weren't surprised at all. They knew he was an unusually emotional man who had always worn his heart on his sleeve. Nor were they surprised when the heart-break quickly turned to outrage and then to raging anger.

'Who are these monsters?' he thundered. 'Bring me my sword and lance, saddle me a horse, I'm at your service, Sir Harry.'

Then, turning to the councillors: 'Gather the men, we'll form a posse and get after these creatures without further ado.'

'A moment, Sir Brian,' Sir Harry said. 'I well understand your anguish and desire to be after these fiends, but Lord Balthazar's strict instructions are that I pursue them alone. What he needs more than anything right now is information. Did anyone see these creatures, either the two with Princess Fleur this morning, or the following two this afternoon?'

'I had reports of horsemen crossing the heath at speed this morning and then again a couple of hours ago,' Sir Brian said. 'Thinking back, it was strange that they skirted the village, but at the time we were all pre-occupied with the festivities, and no-one thought any more of it. It seems clear now that they must have deliberately skirted the village to avoid arousing suspicion.'

'Did you get a description of them?' Sir Harry asked. 'Anything at all?'

'There was one thing,' one of the councillors said. 'It was remarked that their horses looked a little strange.'

'In what way?' Sir Harry asked.

'Two different observers both described them as being unusually small, or at least having unusually short legs.'

'Did they get chance to see the riders?'

'Not really, they were too far away for that, but I can confirm that there were three this morning and two this afternoon.'

'Has anyone seen anything strange in the last few days?' Sir Harry continued. 'Anything out of the ordinary?'

Sir Brian and the councillors looked at each other but agreed there had been nothing.

'Do we know which direction they took?'

'Once the village was behind them, both parties rejoined the Great North Road, and one of the observers reported that the three riders this morning turned into Butterfly Valley.'

'Thank you very much,' Sir Harry said. 'That's very useful information. Now with your leave, Sir Brian, I must pick up their trail.'

'Are you sure there's nothing we can do? It's going to be unbearably frustrating twiddling our thumbs doing nothing while our poor Princess is being swept away by these savages.'

'Be vigilant,' Sir Harry replied. 'We don't know how many more of these beasts are abroad in the kingdom, or what they might be up to. If you see anything strange please send a rider to Lord Balthazar without delay.'

With that, Sir Brian and the councillors accompanied Sir Harry back to his horse and bade him good fortune, as he swept away up the Great North Road.

The news that the creatures had turned into Butterfly Valley suggested they'd be taking the north-west road in the direction of either The Stones, the nearest point at which they could cross the Great West River, or the Snowy Mountains, but where after that was anyone's guess. Sir Harry knew the countryside around the valley like the back of his hand. If he made haste he should be able to head them off and engage them before they got to the other end. A glance at the sun told him he had around two hours before sunset.

The big stallion loved nothing more than a fast gallop and, even though their path took them uphill, they made very good time. Butterfly Valley was broad and shallow at its ends but narrowed into a deep gorge in the middle, and that's where Sir Harry planned to intercept his prey. In little more than an hour he'd reached the southern lip of the gorge, a long rocky ridge. He dismounted, left the horse some distance away and found himself the perfect vantage point. He had a clear view of the valley in both directions and he knew he was hidden from the view of anyone looking up. He took out a long brass telescope and swept the valley towards the east. At first there was nothing, but then two riders came into view. To begin with he couldn't make them out, but as they drew nearer it became clear they were his prey. They were just as described: hideous, mutilated faces and strange, short-legged horses. As they came closer Sir Harry could see they looked big and powerful, and he decided that to try and take on both of them would be too much of a risk. Instead, he'd kill one outright and then engage the other with a view to capturing and interrogating it. He returned to his horse, took his bow from its sheath and returned to his position on the ridge. A single shot to the heart should do the trick, given that there was no armour to get in the way. He waited a few moments until they came into range and then loosed his arrow. As he did so the creature's horse suddenly stumbled on a pebble, causing the arrow to strike home slightly off target. It penetrated deeply into the flesh and knocked the creature from its horse, but it didn't kill it. On seeing this, the second rider immediately turned his horseback down the valley and retreated a hundred paces. Crouching low on his haunches he waited a while, straining his eyes to pick out the bowman. Then, seeing nothing, he stole back to his injured companion. Sir Harry watched them both examine the wound and exchange a few words. Then something unexpected happened. The injured creature lifted himself to a kneeling position, raised his head and his companion smashed his skull with a single mighty blow of his club. He then leapt on his horse and, lying low in the saddle, galloped towards the end of the gorge.

Sir Harry returned to his horse, clicked his heels and galloped along the ridge, taking care to keep the fleeing creature in sight. He had soon overtaken him and was able to make his way down the path towards the mouth of the valley. When the creature emerged from the gorge Sir Harry was already in place with his lance at the ready, the King's colours fluttering in the breeze. On seeing Sir Harry, the creature pulled up sharply, wheeled his horse round and studied the knight carefully, no doubt weighing up his chances in a fight. He must have quickly realised that club against lance amounted to no chance at all, so he peered back down the gorge to consider his chances of escape. Again, the odds were against him. His enemy's horse was clearly the faster beast. The creature must have concluded that fighting was the only option and he raised his club and turned his horse to face his enemy head on. Sir Harry trotted forward a few paces, keeping his lance high, and called out, beckoning the creature to throw down his club and surrender. He held his wrists together to show that he meant to take him prisoner rather than kill him. The creature either didn't understand or didn't trust Sir Harry. With a savage kick to his horse's flanks he spurred it forward, furiously swinging his club around his head. Sir Harry had no alternative other than to lower his lance. He clicked his heels once more and his stallion thundered towards the creature. His lance went right through its chest and tore it from its saddle before it had any chance of bringing that nasty-looking club into play. Sir Harry climbed down from his horse, walked over to the creature and tried to speak with it. All he got in return was a savage, demonic glare and a hissing, spitting reply. The creature died very quickly.

Sir Harry studied both bodies carefully. The description he'd been given was accurate. Muscular and red-skinned with tattooed heads and hideously mutilated faces, but there was nothing on them that might give a clue as to who they were or where they'd come from. He walked over to the horses. They were, indeed, strange beasts. Broad with deep chests and muscular necks and shoulders. Their legs were shorter than usual but appeared to be very strong. Their coats were much thicker and coarser than any he'd seen before and their manes were long. Despite their obvious strength they were skittish beasts and it took Sir Harry a while to get close to them. Once he had, he made a few unusual findings. They wore rudimentary bridles but no stirrups. The saddles were also very basic, and when he removed them he found a leather sack under each one containing raw meat in an advanced state of putrefaction. Attached to one side of the saddle there were strips of dried flesh, which Sir Harry assumed served as their food. On the other side there was a bunch of straws, a leather pouch of liquid which looked like milk but smelt of decaying flesh and a sprig of thick skinned, blood-red berries. Once he was satisfied that there was nothing else of note he secured the two bodies to each of the horses and, mounting his own stallion, led them out of the valley onto the road to Gerard's Ford.

About an hour later he reached the village square. The day's festivities had clearly ended, and only a few candle-lit tables were still occupied. Sir Harry secured his horses and enquired after the village elder, one Master Thomas.

He and his councillors were appalled at the news of Princess Fleur's abduction and, on seeing the creatures, were horrified by their mutilated faces.

'These creatures need to be returned to the Golden Castle and Lord Balthazar as soon as possible,' Sir Harry explained. 'We have to identify them and determine where they've come from. Can you arrange for riders to move out right away?'

'Consider it done,' Master Thomas replied, and he motioned one of his colleagues to arrange it.

'Is there anything else we can do?' he continued. 'Anything at all?'

'I'd be grateful if you could do two things,' Sir Harry replied. 'First I need a fresh mount. This stallion has galloped hard and fast and is all but finished. And second, I need to know if anyone in the village saw riders pass by this morning.'

'They did,' Master Thomas replied, 'several villagers reported three riders galloping across the meadow between the road and stream late this morning.'

'Did they notice anything unusual about them?' Sir Harry asked.

'Nothing, except that they were riding across the meadow rather than along the road through the village.'

'Which direction were they taking?'

'They were riding north, which would take them either to Lord Lupus's tower or, if they turned off, to the Great West River and The Stones.'

'Was anyone able to provide a description?'

'I'm afraid not, they were too far away.'

'Well,' Sir Harry said, bringing the meeting to an end, 'you've been very helpful. Now if you'd be so kind as to bring the fresh mount I'll detain you no longer.'

'Are you sure there's nothing else we can do?' Master Thomas asked.

'Nothing,' Sir Harry replied, 'other than deliver those creatures to Lord Balthazar as soon as possible.'

Sir Harry took his leave of Master Thomas and rode out of Gerard's Ford towards the north. A short way out of the village he slowed down to study the tracks and, as expected, picked up those of the three riders. He looked up to the heavens. The sky was clear, the moon shone brightly and he reckoned he had about two hours before the rains came. So, although fatigue was beginning to creep through his bones, he decided to cover as much distance as he could.

The new stallion was slightly smaller than the last, probably a little younger, but it felt every bit as strong and eager, and within moments they'd settled into an steady gallop which they maintained until, as expected, the rains came, torrential rain which slowed him to a canter.

Having to slow down was frustrating, but it was an opportunity to get some much-needed rest. He reckoned he had at least two more days' solid riding ahead of him and he had no idea what he might find at the end of his journey, so he wrapped his knight's cloak around himself and allowed his mind to rest.

The next day's journey was uneventful. The road took him past four more villages and at each one he got the same message. Three riders had been seen, but always from a distance. Nobody was able to provide a description or any new information. As the shadows lengthened he reached Badger's Bluff, where he changed his horse once more. Again, there was no new information to be had, so he set off at a gallop as he'd done the night before and then, as the rains came, he settled into gentle canter.

The quiet of the road and the steady rhythm of the young horse soon lulled Sir Harry into a shallow slumber and his tired mind began to turn over, time and again, the events of the last two days. Who were these dreadful creatures? Why had they taken Princess Fleur? Where were they taking her? He went over their appearance, the way they spoke, their horses and the things they were carrying:

the dried meat, the rancid milk, the straws and the blood berries. Was there anything that could provide a clue? Then, just as he was about to drift into a deeper sleep, a sudden thought jolted him back. Everyone he'd spoken to from Hare's Heath to Badger's Bluff had reported seeing these three riders. Why hadn't they tried to hide themselves, to pass unnoticed? He couldn't believe it was beyond them to do that. After all, they'd managed to get to Barnaby's Mill without being seen. Could it be that they wanted to be seen, if only from a distance? And if so, why? Sir Harry pondered this for a while and then a terrible thought occurred to him: were these creatures asking to be followed? Could they be decoys luring their pursuers into a dead end, making time for others of their kind to take Princess Fleur in another direction altogether? Were they all being duped? Clearly, he couldn't be sure of this, but his keen tracker's instinct told him that something wasn't quite right. He smelt a rat. The question was, what to do? He was duty bound to follow his orders to the letter and continue his pursuit as far as it would take him but, at the same time, he needed to make his suspicions known to Lord Balthazar as soon as possible.

As he continued north the next morning the scenery began to change. The gentle meadows that had flanked the road since Gerard's Ford were now giving way to wilder, more rugged countryside. By noon he could see the blue waters of Pine Wood Lake and his next stopping point, Jasper's Ferry. This was the point at which the road split. If he carried on north he'd eventually reach Lord Lupus's castle and the Snowy Mountains; if he turned left it would take him to The Stones and the precarious river crossing out of the Golden Kingdom and into the Emerald Forest and beyond.

Sir Harry's enquiries at Jasper's Ferry were met with the now-familiar response. Three riders had been seen late last evening, but only from a distance. They had taken the road to The Stones. Once again, the village elders were utterly appalled by Princess Fleur's abduction and only too eager to provide a fresh new horse. While it was being made ready Sir Harry penned a report to Lord Balthazar, outlining the fears that had assailed him in the night. Once he had sealed the note and watched the two riders set off, he picked up the lake-side road and galloped for The Stones.

For the first couple of hours the road clung to the rocky shore of the lake but then turned away and began to climb steeply into the pine forest which gave the lake its name. As he careered through the trees he soon became aware of a distant thundering which told him he was getting closer to the mighty Great West River. Soon the trees began to thin out and he reached Angler's View, the rocky outcrop which overlooked the river valley. There, in the distance, not an hour's ride away, were The Stones. Sir Harry trained his telescope on the riverbank and carefully followed its course. To begin with there was nothing out of the ordinary, but then his glass fell on a column of knights galloping south at great speed. At first, he couldn't tell who they were, but as they got closer he could make out Lord Lupus's colours. That surprised him. Did it mean that news of Princess Fleur's abduction had already reached Lord Lupus?

Sir Harry guided his horse carefully down the stony slope of the outcrop and galloped towards The Stones. There was now a steady stream of knights, foot soldiers and archers making their way quickly along the riverbank and, right ahead, not far from The Stones, was the unmistakable figure of Lord Lupus. Like Sir Brian, he was a mountain of a man, and appeared to have been wrought from the same solid rock. He was one of the lords of the Four Towers, the King's trusted lieutenants and the Royal authority throughout these parts.

'Sir Harry,' he said, striding over to the knight and helping him down from horse, 'it's good to see you, my friend.'

'It's good to see you, My Lord,' Sir Harry replied, shaking his huge hand. 'I didn't expect to meet you this day. May I ask what brings you to The Stones?'

'The same as you, I'll wager. Come with me, if you please.'

And he led Sir Harry down to the water's edge.

'Three horses, Sir Harry,' he said, pointing, 'and strange-looking beasts they are too.'

'And their riders?' Sir Harry asked.

'Even stranger,' replied Lord Lupus. 'And they're dead. At least two of them are.'

'Which two?' Sir Harry asked anxiously.

'The two ugly devils. We've found no trace of Princess Fleur.'

'So, you know about Princess Fleur?'

'I do, indeed, Sir Harry. A Grey Falcon from Lord Balthazar arrived with the dreadful news and a description of her abductors late yesterday afternoon. We've been travelling south ever since and reached here earlier this afternoon. The horses were by the river, as you see them now, so I assumed the riders had crossed The Stones and I sent men to investigate. They reported that there were no footprints on the far bank so I concluded they must have been swept away by the river. As you know, The Stones are desperately treacherous. I sent riders down the riverbank and, sure enough, about four hundred paces away we found two bodies smashed and broken against the rocks. We continued down the riverbank searching for a sign of Princess Fleur but, so far, there's been no trace of the poor soul.'

'May I see the bodies?' Sir Harry asked.

'Come with me,' Lord Lupus replied, 'they're in the tent.'

They looked just like the two others. Reddish skins, muscular builds and hideously mutilated faces.

'Do you know anything about these creatures?' Sir Harry asked, turning to Lord Lupus.

'Nothing at all, nor do any of my captains. I've sent a rider back to the castle with instructions for the scholars and scribes to search our library and archives. Perhaps they'll find something. Do you know anything?'

'Very little, My Lord,' Sir Harry replied. 'I killed two of them on the way here and had a good look at them before sending the bodies back to Lord Balthazar. I've never seen anything like them before.'

'Is there anything we can learn from the bodies?' Lord Lupus asked.

'I think there's more to be learnt from the horses,' Sir Harry replied. 'As you say, they're strange-looking beasts, but I wonder if the short legs, broad chests and long coats tell of a home that's somewhere in the cold lands to the north? Have you noticed they don't wear shoes? When I was scouting beyond the Snowy Mountains some months ago I came across a caravan of merchant adventurers who told of unusual, un-shod horses favoured by nomads that travel the lands beyond the Ring of Fire.'

'Interesting,' Lord Lupus said, striding back to look at the horses.

'And look,' Sir Harry said, lifting one of the horse's manes. 'What do you see?'

'Scars,' Lord Lupus said, 'small scars.'

'Indeed,' Sir Harry continued, 'I'd say they're puncture marks made by these straws.' And he showed Lord Lupus the straws that hung from the saddle next to the dried meat.'

'What does it mean, Sir Harry?'

'I can't be sure, My Lord, but my guess is that these creatures live off their horses' blood as well as their meat and milk. That suggests a high level of dependence on their horses, which brings us back to the possibility that they're nomads, perhaps the nomads the merchants spoke of.'

'But what on earth would nomads want with Princess Fleur?' Lord Lupus asked.

'I can't imagine,' Sir Harry replied, and as they continued to discuss the possibilities, one of the captains returned from along the riverbank.

'My Lord,' he said, 'we've been down as far as the Dragon's Mouth gorge, and we've found nothing, absolutely nothing.'

Sir Harry looked at Lord Lupus. 'I don't think you will find anything,' he said. 'My guess is that Princess Fleur is miles away from here.'

'What do you mean?' Lord Lupus asked, somewhat perplexed.

And Sir Harry told him his theory about being lured in the wrong direction.

'Right,' Lord Lupus said, when Sir Harry had finished, 'this is what we must do. You must write a report setting out everything you've just told me about the creatures, where you think they're from and your belief that Princess Fleur will not be found in these parts. I will endorse your theory and I'll send a Grey Falcon to Lord Balthazar right away. And you, Sir Harry, must return to the Golden Castle at once. I believe your skills and instinct as a scout and tracker may prove invaluable in helping to find our Princess, and Lord Balthazar will certainly need them.'

'Indeed, My Lord, can you provide a fresh horse?'

'Consider it done,' Lord Lupus replied, and he motioned the captain to prepare two horses. If Sir Harry was to get back to the castle as quickly as possible, he'd need a spare mount.

A short while later Sir Harry took his leave of Lord Lupus and set off back along the path that had brought him here. He stopped on the edge of the bluff and looked back towards the river. The tent had already been taken down and an ever-lengthening column was on the move. Lord Lupus had explained that despite their findings that afternoon, and Sir Harry's theories, nothing was yet certain, so he'd continue to follow his orders. He would meet with Lord Orcus further down the river and together they'd start to draw the net in towards the Golden Castle.

4

THE BRIEFING ROOM

The days following Princess Fleur's abduction were terrible. The festivities that had been planned for Midsummer's evening were replaced by an outpouring of grief and a torch-lit vigil in the courtyard outside the palace. People of all ages volunteered to take to the road and run down the creatures that had taken their Princess. And when her classmates returned from Barnaby's Mill the next morning, and the full savagery of the attack and the horror of her abductors became known, the entire castle was seized by an anger that Lord Balthazar had never seen before.

Hardest hit was the Royal Family itself. As the horrible realisation that they may never see their beloved daughter again began to sink in the Queen was inconsolable. Even with potions prepared by Lord Balthazar she was unable to eat or sleep and was never far from tears. Princess Hannah drew on all her strength to try and console her mother, but she too was in the grip of a terrible fear and needed all the support that Sir Alfred could give her. The King never gave in to tears but in his stomach, he felt the grip of some icy hand twisting and turning. He passed every hour of the day and night with the professors and scribes, poring over books, scrolls and letters in search of a clue that might help him bring his daughter back. And when his eyes grew too heavy with fatigue to continue reading, he could be seen pacing the battlements, one moment looking into the distance, as if searching for his daughter, the next head bowed down in despair.

Lord Balthazar had drafted every professor, scholar, librarian, teacher, secretary and scribe in the castle into the search and had organised them into teams, each with its own area of focus. Every hour the team leaders reported back to him, but despite this enormous effort they couldn't find anything about these creatures or where they were from.

Lord Balthazar also enlisted the thousands of well-wishers who'd joined in the vigil, and over the following two days they scoured the land all around Barnaby's Mill. Not a stone remained unturned, but every report was the same. Not a trace of the creatures could be found, nor any clue as to where they'd come from or where they might be taking Princess Fleur.

Lord Balthazar received several updates from Sir Harry and he eagerly awaited the bodies of the creatures he'd killed in Butterfly Valley, but so far, the reports hadn't added much to the little they already knew. What they needed more than anything right now was confirmation that the lords of the Four Towers had connected and started drawing in the dragnet.

Later that afternoon Lord Balthazar retired to his study in the Great Tower to examine a work of Geography that had been discovered by one of the scholars working in the darkest recesses of the library. It was entitled *Travels Beyond the Flames* by one Master John of Beavers' Lodge. Beavers' Lodge was an ancient village which still nestled in the foothills of the Snowy Mountains, and Master John had been an intrepid adventurer and explorer of the lands beyond the Ring of Fire. Even though the book was several hundred years old Lord Balthazar hoped it might reveal something of value. He was determined that not a single stone should be left unturned.

Just as he was about to settle into his reading there was a knock at the door and his secretary, Master Melchior, hurried in.

'My Lord,' he said, 'a Grey Falcon has arrived,' and he handed Lord Balthazar a tightly rolled scroll bearing Lord Lupus's seal.

Lord Balthazar opened it and read Sir Harry's report.

'Inform His Majesty that we've had word from Lord Lupus and Sir Harry. I'll see him in His Briefing Room in half an hour.'

'Am I to summon the Council of Elders, My Lord?'

'No, we don't have time, just the King and Queen, and Princess Hannah and Sir Alfred.'

'Very good, My Lord.'

'Your Majesties,' Lord Balthazar began, as soon as everyone had gathered in the Briefing Room, 'the bodies of the two creatures we believe to be responsible for abducting Princess Fleur were fished from the Great West River yesterday afternoon. There was no third body.'

'Thank heavens for that,' the Queen said with a huge sigh of relief.

'An extensive search along the bank has found no trace of Princess Fleur,' Lord Balthazar continued.

'Then what's happened to her?' asked the King. 'Where is she?'

'We don't know, My Lord, but Sir Harry believes that she was never with those creatures.'

'But she was seen with them, every report he sent confirmed that.'

'They confirmed three horses, My Lord, but nobody got close enough to actually identify the riders. The sightings were always from a distance. Sir Harry believes that the two creatures we've been following tricked us into thinking they had Princess Fleur while, in fact, she's been carried off in some other direction. In other words, he believes we've been led on a wild goose chase.'

'Which direction?' asked the Queen. 'Where have they taken her?'

'At the moment, My Lady, we don't know, but Sir Harry believes he may have found some clues. He caught up with the two creatures that left Barnaby's Mill after the coaches arrived to collect the children, and he killed them both in Butterfly Valley. The bodies and their horses are on the way back to me as we speak. But before releasing the bodies he made some important observations which are outlined in his report.'

'What does he say?' Sir Alfred asked.

'That the horses and the few items he found on them suggest the creatures could be nomads from the lands beyond the Ring of Fire.'

'Nomads, what would nomads want with Princess Fleur?' the King asked, with a tone of exasperation in his voice. 'And what on earth are nomads doing in the Golden Kingdom?'

'We don't know,' Lord Balthazar replied.

'How much faith can we put in Sir Harry's words?' the King asked.

'Sir Harry is the very best ranger and tracker we've had for many years. He's an acute observer of men and nature and has a sound instinct. It is for good reason that he's become known to many as the Bloodhound. Of course, we can't be sure he's right but, in the absence of any other information, I think this is the best theory we have.'

'So, what do we do now?' the Queen asked. 'We still don't know where they're taking my daughter or why.' And she broke down into tears once more.

'What's your counsel, My Lord?' the King asked, turning to Lord Balthazar. 'Should we instruct Lord Aguila to double back and start searching the Ring of Fire?'

'I think not, Your Majesty. Lord Aguila should have connected with Lord Drago by now and I think we should draw the net in, as planned. My guess is that Princess Fleur is still in the Golden Kingdom and while that's the case we have every chance of finding her.'

'And what are we to do in the meantime?' the Queen asked through her tears. 'Continue sitting on our backsides doing nothing?'

'It's a fair question, My Lord,' the King said, looking to Lord Balthazar. 'We can't wait anymore. We all need to be doing something, and fast.'

Lord Balthazar understood the anguish and frustration

everyone was feeling. His difficulty was that, for once, he didn't know what the best course of action was. Sir Harry's observations had shed vital light on these creatures and where they might be heading, but they were hardly blueprints for action. The last thing he wanted was to send everyone off on another wild goose chase. However, he recognised that direct action would give people a sense of purpose and lift morale.

'I agree, My Lord,' he said. 'My advice is that we send the Companions to the Ring of Fire. I propose that Sir Miles takes command. I'll brief him in my Tower as soon as we're finished here and instruct him to move out immediately.'

Then, with the burning eyes of a warrior, he turned to the Queen.

'My Lady,' he said, 'these foul creatures have driven a red-hot blade into your heart and the hearts of all of us. On Midsummer's evening there was an outpouring of grief the like of which I've never seen before. That grief has now turned to anger and an irresistible determination to bring our Princess back. Every man, woman and child has answered the call to action. The Golden Kingdom will not fail you. Our Princess will be returned to her family and her people, and these devils, whoever they are, will pay the most dreadful price.'

'Thank you for those kind words,' the Queen replied through her tears. 'You must excuse me now.'

As Princess Hannah helped her mother from the table, the door burst open and another messenger hurried over to Lord Balthazar with a note. Lord Balthazar read it quickly, then threw back his head and heaved a huge sigh of relief.

'Wait, Your Highness,' he called. 'We have a positive sighting. Princess Fleur's alive. She's been spotted. She crossed the Great East River at King's Crossing two days ago.'

'Go on,' the Queen cried, rushing back to the table.

'The letter's from Lord Aguila,' Lord Balthazar said, adjusting his spectacles. 'Allow me to read it.'

And as the Queen returned to her place at the table he began to read:

'My Lord,

'By the time this report reaches you a day will have passed since our column reached King's Crossing.

'We arrived, around lunchtime, and immediately summoned the crossing guard, explained our mission and asked if anything had been seen either of Princess Fleur or her abductors. This is what they reported: two men and a young child had arrived at the ferry the previous afternoon and demanded immediate passage to the far bank. The guards described all three as being dressed in desert attire: flowing robes and hoods, but they did manage to get a good look at them. They described the men as being tall and red-skinned. However, they didn't have any signs of the facial mutilations you described. We pressed them on this point, but they were all clear: there were no facial mutilations or disfigurements, nor was there any disguise. They described the child as being a girl, around seven years old, with long brown hair. She too had a reddish complexion but was very dirty and appeared to have been crying.'

At this point both the Queen and Princess Hannah broke down again. The King asked Lord Balthazar to wait while he and Sir Alfred gave the ladies what little comfort they could.

'My poor, poor darling,' the Queen kept repeating through her tears, but after a few moments she gathered herself and nodded to Lord Balthazar to continue.

'The guards observed that the girl's tears had washed away some of the dirt and redness, suggesting the latter was some kind of makeup. That raised their suspicions and they scrutinised the girl more closely. They observed that underneath her robes she was wearing a red T-shirt and pumps, clothes not usually worn by the desert folk. They asked the men where they'd come from and where they were going. They spoke our language and explained that they were merchants who visited the Golden Castle every year for the Midsummer fair and were now on their way to another fair in the Kingdom of Alcazar. The child, they said, was exhausted by the journey and had become ill with the food she'd eaten. The guards tried to speak with her directly, but it appeared she was, indeed, too tired and unwell to reply.'

Again, Lord Balthazar had to pause to give the Queen time to overcome the distress the account was clearly causing her. At length he continued.

'One of the men showed the guards a half-empty bottle of medicine and explained it was that which was making the girl sleepy. That satisfied the guards. They said that although the travellers were unusual, there was no reason to doubt their words. Strangers are common at King's Crossing and there was nothing to make them think the girl had been kidnapped, or that she was Princess Fleur. They granted the travellers passage on the next ferry and the ferryman saw them alight on the far bank late in the afternoon.

'On hearing this news, I ordered a company of men to pick up the trail and follow the creatures into the desert. As I write, I have not had any news from them. I am now awaiting the arrival of Lord Drago, at which point, I will continue with my orders and advance towards the Golden Castle.

'Your faithful Servant,

'Lord Aguila.'

'So, my darling's been dragged off into the desert?' the Queen wailed.

'Can we be certain it was Fleur?' the King asked, as he and Princess Hannah tried to steady and calm the Queen.

'No, we can't be certain,' Lord Balthazar replied, 'but the description fits.'

'What about the creatures she was with?' the King continued. 'They didn't have the same facial mutilations as the others, or speak with the same snake-like hissing or snarling. It appears they speak our language.'

'I believe we should assume it *was* Princess Fleur,' Lord Balthazar said.

'Did you send a falcon to King's Crossing?' the King asked. 'Did the Captain of the Guard know that Fleur had been taken?'

'I did not, My Lord, I sent falcons to the lords of the four towers and put my faith in operation dragnet. I believed we would seal the kingdom well before these creatures could reach a border. Clearly I was mistaken.'

'So what happens now?' the Queen asked.

'I suggest we get after Princess Fleur without delay. I propose to lead the pursuit myself.'

'Good,' replied the King. 'Let's make ready.'

Lord Balthazar turned to Princess Hannah and Sir Alfred.

'I would like you two to come with me. You both have special skills which may prove vital. I propose we move out within the hour. Princess Hannah, please make yourself ready. Sir Alfred, come with me to the tower.'

They all took their leave of the King and Queen, and Lord Balthazar led Sir Alfred to his office.

'We will proceed with a small party,' he said, 'speed is of the essence.'

'Just the three of us?' Sir Alfred asked.

'No, four of us,' Lord Balthazar replied. 'I want Sir Luca, as well. You'll inform him as soon as we're finished here.'

'What about Sir Harry and the Companions?' Sir Alfred asked. 'Don't you think the Companions would be better employed coming with us rather than heading for the Ring of Fire?'

'If Sir Harry were here, he'd be coming with us; his skills are invaluable. However, he's not due back for some time and we can't afford to wait for him. Since we don't know our final destination, I don't want him to try and follow us. I want him to go with the Companions to the Ring of Fire.'

'And what is our destination, My Lord?'

'Our immediate destination is King's Crossing. We'll pick up the trail there. These creatures won't be going to Alcazar, we can be sure of that, but they may well be heading for Endora's Pool.'

'What makes you say that, My Lord?'

'Whatever their final destination, they'll have to cross the desert, which means they'll need plenty of water and provisions. Endora's Pool is the place where everyone stocks up.'

'Do you think we'll be able to catch up with them there, My Lord?'

'I very much doubt it, Sir Alfred, they've got too much of a lead over us.'

'Where do you think they'll make for after Endora's Pool?'

'I'm not sure, but if Sir Harry's right, I think they'll be heading north. If I'm not mistaken, there'll be plenty of characters hanging around Endora's Pool only too happy to point us in the right direction, for a small fee, of course.'

'Will we be able to trust them, My Lord?'

'Some yes, others no, so we'll need to be very careful. The creatures may have bribed people to feed us false information, and we know they're masters at disguising their tracks and throwing followers off the scent. However, there is something else we can do. Before we set off I'm going to send a Grey Falcon to Lord Zubin at Alcazar and ask him to comb the desert with the magic carpet. If he can oblige, we may yet be able to turn the tables on these beasts.'

'If we go north from Endora's Pool what are we likely to find?' Sir Harry asked.

'That's the big question,' Lord Balthazar replied. 'Let me show you what we do know,' and he took Sir Alfred over to an enormous map that hung on the wall at the far side of the room.

'This is a map of the desert lands between the Great East River and the Kingdom of Alcazar. As you can see,' he said, tapping the map with a long wooden pointer, 'this is the Great East River and right up here, to the right of it we have the end of the Snake's Back Mountains, a massive mountainous ridge which stretches off the map into the far north. Further to the east are the Flaming Mountains, another huge range which stretches along the edge of the Northern Desert, way beyond Alcazar. And if you look here, just below the gap between the Snake's Head and the Flaming Mountains, there's an area coloured orange rather than the yellow that normally denotes desert. It's known in Alcazar as the Giant's Shoulder and is said to be the hottest and most treacherous desert on earth. Unless the creatures know a way through the mountains, this may well be the route they planned to take.'

'Do you know what's beyond the Giant's Shoulder?' Sir Alfred asked.

'No,' Lord Balthazar replied. 'The map stops there. No-one knows what's beyond. It's never been charted.'

Lord Balthazar brought his brief geography lesson to an end, showed Sir Alfred to the door, and returned to his desk to write scrolls to Lord Zubin and the lords of the Four Towers. He gave Sir Miles his orders, instructed Master Melchior and his team of scribes on how to safely go about searching the catacombs, and he removed the seals. He then gathered a few belongings for the journey, bade farewell to Master Melchior and went to join his travelling companions in the courtyard.

5

ENDORA'S POOL

The four riders set off from the Golden Castle at a gallop. Lord Balthazar's plan was to ride night and day and reach Endora's Pool the following evening. He reckoned the creatures were three days ahead of them and probably had already left Endora's Pool by now. His hope was not to catch up with them but to find someone who had seen them and the direction they'd taken. He knew that people didn't stay long at the oasis; they stocked up with provisions, rested and were quickly on their way again. So, the sooner they could get there, the more likely it was they'd find someone able to help.

In the early evening, they made good progress but, as night fell, the clouds gathered and the rain began to fall. As expected, progress was reduced to a gentle canter. There was very little conversation. Everyone had been living on their nerves since Princess Fleur's abduction, and no-one had been able to get any sleep. Princess Hannah was the first to succumb to the rhythm of the road and very quickly she slipped into a dreamless sleep. The two knights lasted a little longer. They turned over in their minds everything they knew about the creatures: their appearance, their size, their brutality and how Sir Harry had prevailed over them with such apparent ease. Eventually, they too gave in to fatigue and slept.

For Lord Balthazar, there was no such escape. He felt the abduction of Princess Fleur very deeply. He'd been close to her since birth and had watched her grow into the loving and vivacious child she now was. He also felt the King and Queen's anguish and was pained by his own helplessness. On top of all that, he was acutely aware that he'd made mistakes. His network of eyes and ears throughout the land had failed to pick up the arrival of these creatures; he'd allowed himself to be drawn into a wild goose chase that only the wisdom of Sir Harry had brought to an end; and operation dragnet, onto which he had pinned his hopes, had failed miserably. All those failures were his. He felt as though he'd personally let down the King and Queen, and the whole kingdom, in its hour of greatest need. And most worrying of all was the realisation that he was no closer to knowing who these creatures were, why they'd taken Princess Fleur or where they were taking her. Some time ago he'd felt a similar helplessness when Princess Hannah had succumbed to the evil magic hidden in her hairbrush. On that occasion, Lord Zubin and Alcazar had come to the rescue. Would they be able to do so again? Lord Balthazar racked his brain and searched the depths of his memory for answers but to no avail. His night was long and painful, and his relentless search for answers was punctuated by painful images and memories of the lovely little child he cared so much for. He felt truly desperate in his hopelessness but was eventually rescued by the first light.

Princess Hannah's deep sleep, the first in days, had eased the weight of despair a little, and as the sun rose, so did her hopes. It was she who set the pace towards King's Crossing. The road was quiet and they made good progress. They stopped at a number of villages to change horses and see if there was any information to be had about Princess Fleur or the creatures. But the response was always the same. If they had passed that way, nobody had seen them, and they'd left no trace.

They reached King's Crossing in the late afternoon, slightly ahead of schedule, and were welcomed by the Captain of the Guard and Lords Aguila and Drago. Lord Balthazar had the Captain summon the guards who'd questioned the two creatures. He got them to repeat every last detail of the encounter, particularly their description of the girl and her state of health. Their account matched exactly the one they'd given Lord Aguila and, after a brief conversation, Lord Balthazar and Princess Hannah agreed that the girl was, indeed, Fleur.

'My Lord Balthazar,' Lord Aguila said, 'if we're sure the girl is Princess Fleur, and that she's being carried across the desert as we speak, wouldn't it make sense to abandon operation dragnet and put all our energies into getting after her without delay? Lord Drago and I are ready to move at your command.'

'What you say makes a lot of sense,' Lord Balthazar replied, 'and I thank you, but right now speed is critical and I'm not sure a large force would be able to move as quickly as our small band. Also, I'm worried that there may be other creatures at large in the Golden Kingdom bent on further mischief. So, for those reasons I'd like you and Lord Drago to proceed with operation dragnet as planned.'

After the two lords had taken their leave, the Captain of the Guard escorted Lord Balthazar and his companions down to the jetty and the waiting ferry.

It was a short journey across the lazy waters of the Great East River, and then a long ride across the desert. The first half of the journey was across hard salt flats. There was very little vegetation or drifting sand to slow the horses down, nor any rain so, with the stars to guide them and a gentle breeze in their faces, they made good progress in relative comfort.

By the following morning the terrain had changed. The wide open flats of the night before had been replaced with a sea of undulating golden dunes. Beautiful to behold but dreadful to traverse, and very soon the horses, ill-suited to travelling across sand, were reduced to a slow plod. By mid-morning the sun was beating down fiercely, and the riders knew the afternoon heat would be difficult to bear. Princess Hannah wondered how on earth her little sister had managed. She just hoped that her desert robes had provided enough protection and that her captors had given her water.

Towards the end of the afternoon the four exhausted riders trudged slowly to the ridge at the top of a great dune and, at last, below them, in the distance, was Endora's Pool, the greatest oasis, crossroads and trading post in the desert.

From a distance, the oasis was like a long green ribbon

of palm trees running along the base of a massive sandstone cliff. The great pool was hidden from view between the palms and the rock, but two smaller pools were visible, nestling in the cliff face. A waterfall fell from one to the other and then cascaded down to the great pool. It was said that on quiet, windless days the sound of the water could be heard from far away, bringing tears of joy to the eyes of many a thirsty and weary traveller.

The journey from the ridge was all downhill, and sensing water ahead of them, the horses found a second wind and their strides lengthened. As they drew closer they could see a thousand tents dotted between the palms and, all around them, a milling throng of people: travellers and merchants from every corner of the world along with their many beasts of burden: camels, horses, donkeys and even teams of desert dogs.

As they rode between the palms, they were struck by the huge variety of tents, and the even greater variety of faces: the dark leathery faces of the marshland people from the south, the sun-cracked cheeks of the desert nomads and the hawk-like appearance of the folks who made their homes in the foothills of the Flaming Mountains. A thousand voices carried on the gentle breeze, some loud and harsh, others soft and gentle. A few spoke the language of the Golden Kingdom and Alcazar, but many conversed in strange, unknown tongues from distant lands.

They passed groups of men reclining on cushions, smoking strange pipes as they listened to storytellers recounting tall tales of heroic deeds and narrow escapes. Others were engrossed in talk of the falcons and sight hounds that accompanied them on their journeys. Proud eagles preened themselves on tall, wooden poles erected next to the tents, while hooded falcons perched on their masters' arms, and long-legged hounds sprawled amongst the cushions. All trusted companions which brought desert quail and hares for the pot.

Some travellers preferred to indulge themselves in the more intimate gossip of the desert and talked in whispers as they cooked their meals, sipped strange drinks and played Kings or Scorpions, or some other game of skill or chance.

For Princess Hannah, Endora's Pool never failed to evoke the romance of adventure, and looking into these strange faces she couldn't help wondering where they'd come from, where they were going or what stories they had to tell. She also knew they were watching her every step. Eyes that pretended to watch the quail turning on the spit, or contemplate the next move on the King's board, were really watching the new arrivals. Where were they from? Where were they going? Were they friend or foe? What was absolutely certain was that, very soon, their presence would be known to everyone. That was the way of the oasis. It was a great crossroads of travellers and goods, but also of news and rumour.

No sooner had they reached the great pool and begun to refresh themselves with its cool, clear water than Sir Alfred alerted them to three men striding purposefully towards them. They wore flowing white robes gathered at the waist by broad black belts and were armed with long curved scimitars. Their faces were covered by the white scarf worn by many of the desert folk to protect their faces from the wind and sun. As they drew nearer Sir Luca stepped forward and clasped his fingers firmly round the hilt of his sword.

'I'll take the one if front,' he said to Sir Alfred, 'you and Lord Balthazar take the others.'

But just as they were about to draw their swords, the man in front flung back his scarf and held out his arms.

'Sir Alfred,' he called, without breaking his stride, 'it's me, Prince Omar. I can't believe you're about to show me your sword?'

Sir Alfred burst into laughter. 'Forgive me, Your Highness,' he said, 'I didn't recognise you in the dark.'

After the two friends had embraced Sir Alfred turned to Sir Luca and said: 'At ease, my friend, you don't want to lock horns with this one, he's the finest swordsman from here to the rising sun. Let me introduce his Royal Highness, Prince Omar of Alcazar.'

After shaking hands with Sir Luca, Prince Omar spotted Princess Hannah. He stepped towards her, gently took her hand and bowed deeply.

'My dearest Princess,' he said, 'it is an honour and great joy to see you again, you look as beautiful as ever, I trust you're well?'

'Thank you, Your Highness,' Princess Hannah replied. 'I'm as well as can be expected in these dreadful circumstances.'

'Indeed, My Lady,' Prince Omar said. 'Allow me say how deeply saddened the whole of Alcazar is to hear this terrible news about Princess Fleur.'

'Thank you for your kind thoughts, Your Highness.'

'And may I add,' he continued, 'that we are greatly angered. I bring a solemn promise from the King and

Queen themselves that our entire kingdom and all its resources are at your disposal. We will do anything in our power to help you bring Princess Fleur back to her family.'

These kind words brought a tear to Princess Hannah's eyes and, as Sir Alfred went to comfort her, Prince Omar turned to Lord Balthazar.

'It's good to see you, My Lord, I trust you, too, are in good health?'

'As always, Your Highness. A little older and stiffer in the bones, perhaps, but, yes, I'm well.'

'My Lord, we received your message two days ago. The magic carpet is at your disposal for as long as you need it. It's beyond the headland and I suggest we all spend the night there, secure from prying eyes and eavesdroppers. We have much to discuss and critical plans to make. But before I show you aboard, is there anything we need to do here in the camp?'

'There is one crucial task we need to perform,' replied Lord Balthazar. 'We need to find out if there's anyone here who saw Princess Fleur and the creatures.'

'It's already been done, My Lord,' Prince Omar replied. 'We knew time would be critical, so the moment we arrived we made enquiries. The good news is that Princess Fleur and the creatures were seen. They stayed at the oasis for just one night, making camp beyond the palms, and stocked up with an unusually large number of water flasks. They left the following morning heading in a northerly direction.'

'Can we be sure that the people who gave you that information were speaking the truth, that they hadn't been bribed by the creatures into misleading us and sending us in the wrong direction?'

'My Lord, it was a merchant and his son who gave us the information. They're from Turfana, one of the ancient wool-spinning communities that make their homes in the foothills of the Flaming Mountains. We've traded with his people for generations and come to esteem them as craftsmen and trust them as merchants. My heart tells me he's told us the truth. However, to make doubly sure we took him and his son for a ride on the carpet and impressed upon them that if they had misled us in any way they would escape neither our eyes nor the talons of our eagles. After seeing their reaction, my head, as well as my heart, tells me we can trust them.'

'I wouldn't doubt your judgement for a moment,' Lord Balthazar replied.

'Then, my friends, allow me to escort you to the magic carpet.'

Princess Hannah, Sir Alfred and, of course, Lord Balthazar had flown the magic carpet before and knew what to expect, but for Sir Luca it was a new experience and as they rounded the end of the rock he was astonished by the sight before him. The carpet, floating a few feet above the ground, was much bigger than he'd expected, almost as big as the tiltyard at the Golden Castle. A hundred lamps twinkled at its corners and along each edge. Prince Omar led them up an invisible stairway, something that Sir Luca wasn't very comfortable about at all, and they were welcomed aboard by the Captain of the Carpeteers, a huge bearded man, dressed in the white robes of state and a huge sky-blue turban. He led them to the centre of the carpet where, beneath a crimson canopy, there were piles upon piles of luxurious silken cushions of every colour imaginable. Once the guests had been settled comfortably, the Captain ordered dinner and snapped his fingers. The carpet rose magically and soundlessly into the air and settled a hundred feet above the oasis.

Princess Hannah could never resist rushing to the edge of the carpet and leaning over the invisible railings to watch the world passing by below, and tonight was no exception. For a few moments, before re-joining her companions, she watched the great pool shimmering in the moonlight and the flickering campfires they'd passed between just a short while before.

Dinner was a mountain of desert quail cooked in delicate sauces and served with the freshest of bread. It was followed by exotic fruits and sweets and, of course, the delicious lemonade for which Alcazar was famous. However, this wasn't the time for extravagance or over-indulgence. As Prince Omar had said, there was much to be discussed and plans to be made so, as soon as the Carpeteers had cleared everything away, they all got down to business.

'Do you know anything about these creatures?' Princess Hannah asked Prince Omar.

'I'm afraid not, My Lady,' he replied. 'As soon as we got your message Lord Zubin summoned the Council of the Wise to see if anyone could shed any light on who they might be, but the short answer was no. Lord Zubin ordered a search of our entire archive, which continues as we speak and, if I know Lord Zubin, he won't rest until he has some answers. But at the time I left, nothing whatsoever had been found about the creatures. I believe that Lord Zubin was also planning to summon the Guild of Merchants, people who have spent their lives travelling the desert, and whose ancestors did the same. Our hope is that there may be someone amongst them who can tell us something.'

'What do you know of the lands beyond the mountains?' Princess Hannah continued.

'Again, My Lady, there's very little I can say. As you know, a burning desert and an enormous barrier of rock separates our world from the one beyond. Merchants and adventurers travel freely within the lands we call our world, and we know a great deal of its peoples and cultures, but nobody attempts to penetrate that barrier and we know very little of what lies beyond.'

'Is it true that the City of the Dead lies somewhere beyond the mountains?' Sir Alfred asked.

'I believe so,' Prince Omar replied, 'but I don't know much about it. I think Lord Balthazar knows much more than I.'

'I'm not sure about that,' Lord Balthazar replied. 'The little I do know was told to me by Lord Zubin. Some say it was built many thousands of years ago by a race of people called "the enemy". Legend has it that they were a proud and cruel people who were forever making war on their neighbours. It's said that one war resulted in a crushing defeat and they were driven from their land. From that moment, their hatred of everyone and everything grew stronger and stronger and they put all their energies into creating an evil magic with which to destroy the people that had defeated them and driven them away. However, the legend tells us that their success didn't last long. They disappeared from the pages of history and their city fell into ruins.'

'Could the creatures have anything to do with the "enemy"?' Princess Hannah asked. 'Could they be taking my sister to the City of the Dead?'

'It's possible, My Lady,' Lord Balthazar replied. 'We just don't know.'

'The one thing we do know,' Prince Omar said, 'is that they're heading for the Giant's Shoulder. As soon as we'd spoken with the merchant and his son, we took the carpet north to see if we could pick up their trail. Unfortunately, severe sandstorms rendered that impossible, but we did stop a few caravans travelling north-east towards the Flaming Mountains. None of them had seen or heard of the creatures heading in that direction, so I think we can say with some certainty that they headed due north.'

'Then that's the way we must go,' Princess Hannah said. 'We must get all the water flasks we need and set off for the Giant's Shoulder at first light.'

6

THE GIANT'S SHOULDER

They left Endora's Pool just before dawn the following morning. The plan was to fly as near to the Giant's Shoulder as they could before dusk, camp overnight and then take the first step into the unknown the next day. By mid-day they'd reached Mustapha's Finger, one of the northern desert's most famous landmarks. It was a huge pillar of rock which towered above the sand and looked as though it was pointing at the sun like a crooked, stony finger. According to legend the finger belonged to Mustapha, an intrepid merchant who once travelled between the desert folk and the people beyond the mountains. It's said that one day he lost his way in a terrible sandstorm and an evil djinn stole his water. Within hours he'd succumbed to the burning sun and in his death throes and his fury, he shook his finger at the sun, blaming it for summoning the djinn that killed him. For desert travellers, Mustapha's Finger has always been a vital signpost, marking the point at which they should make their turn north-east towards the Flaming Mountains. It was also the halfway point between Endora's Pool and the Giant's Shoulder.

By mid-afternoon the sun was beating down more fiercely than ever and the gentle breeze which had cooled Princess Hannah that morning was now beginning to burn her cheeks. The view was unchanging: an endless sea of golden sand under a blue, cloudless sky. In time, the snow-capped peaks of the Flaming Mountains began to slowly shimmer into view above the distant horizon and Princess Hannah noticed that two of the carpeteers had called the Captain and Prince Omar and were pointing excitedly into the sky. She hurried over to see what they were looking at.

'Have you seen something?' she asked anxiously.

'We have, My Lady,' Prince Omar replied. 'Look,' he said, pointing to the sky, 'it's Storm Larks. They're heading south.'

'What does that mean?' Princess Hannah asked, having never heard of Storm Larks before.

'When Storm Larks fly south it's a clear sign that a storm's on its way.'

And within moments the wind began to pick up dramatically and start to buffet and toss them. The Captain ordered everyone away from the edges of the carpet and on to the cushions in the middle.

'My Lords and Lady,' he said, 'as you can see, we've had a sudden change of weather. That's quite normal for this part of the world, and nothing to be worried about. The desert is an unpredictable place, especially the northern desert. Provided it doesn't worsen, I propose we continue on our current course and get you as near to the Giant's Shoulder as we can.'

'What happens if it worsens?' Sir Alfred asked.

'If the wind gets too strong we'll have to turn back and wait until it dies down and is safe enough to continue. If we continue into the eye of the storm there's a risk of capsizing the carpet and killing everyone on board. But for now, it's safe to go on.'

'How far are we from the Shoulder?' Lord Balthazar asked.

'If we continue at this rate we should be there within two hours, a little ahead of schedule,' the Captain replied.

'Then let's make what haste we can,' Prince Omar said, 'and see how far we get. Remember, desert storms often die as quickly as they appear.'

The Captain left his passengers in the relative safety of the cushions and joined his crew at the front of the carpet. For the next hour there was no change. The storm continued to buffet and toss the carpet but no more than before. However, as they drew closer to the Giant's Shoulder it began to get much worse and started throwing them violently from side to side.

'My Lords and Lady,' the Captain said, returning to the cushions, 'I'm afraid we can't go any further, the storm is getting too bad. I suggest we turn around immediately and put down further south.'

'How far are we from the Shoulder now?' Princess Hannah asked.

'Less than an hour away, My Lady, but the wind's getting so strong, it's slowing us down to a crawl. There's a real chance we're going to buckle and capsize. We have to turn round.'

'We can't turn round now,' Princess Hannah replied. 'Not when we're so close. Can you set us down here and we'll go the rest of the way on foot?'

'I can, My Lady,' the Captain replied, 'but I must advise that in these conditions it would be far too dangerous. You'd be fighting against a driving wind in searing heat. Fatigue and dehydration would quickly overcome you, as they do even the strongest and most experienced of desert travellers. Disorientation and death would follow swiftly. If you insist on being set down here you'll need to take immediate shelter and wait until the storm dies down before moving on.'

'How long will the storm last?' Princess Hannah asked.

'It's impossible to say, My Lady. Sometimes they're gone in a matter of moments, sometimes they last for days before blowing themselves out.'

'The Captain's right, My Lady,' Prince Omar said. 'If we alight now we must make camp and wait.'

'Your Highness,' Princess Hannah replied, 'I'm sure you're right. You and the Captain know far more about the desert and its storms than I do. In normal circumstances, I'd bow to your better judgement without a moment's hesitation. But these are not normal circumstances. As we speak, monstrous creatures are dragging my little sister to an unknown land, and who knows what dreadful fate. I simply will not sit around waiting for this storm to die out. You may all camp here if you wish, but I must go on. Captain, please prepare to take the carpet down.'

'I'm coming with you, My Lady,' Sir Alfred said without a moment's hesitation.

'We're all coming with you,' Lord Balthazar added.

'Captain, I'd be obliged if you'd take the carpet down as Princess Hannah asks.'

'Your wish is my command, My Lord.'

With that the Captain and his crew threw themselves into the task of holding the carpet in one piece as they brought it down to the ground. As soon as they were down everyone, except the Captain and his crew, clambered off, struggling desperately to hold on to their gear and the panicking horses. Eventually they were all down and, as the carpet turned away to the south, they braced themselves against the wind and stinging sand, and set off towards the Shoulder. Every step was a desperate battle against the elements. Princess Hannah felt as though she was being held back by an enormous invisible hand, while the wind burned through her desert robes. Very quickly she understood what the Captain had meant about fatigue and dehydration, and she began to wonder how long she could carry on. But quite suddenly the wind began to drop, the restraining hand loosened its grip and the intensity of the burning died down a little. As the sand began to settle, visibility improved and ahead of them they could see a long avenue of strange pillars, each very similar to Mustapha's Finger.

'What in the world are those?' Princess Hannah asked.

'They're good news, My Lady,' Prince Omar replied. 'Legend has it that when you see those pillars you know you're not far from the Giant's Shoulder. Welcome, my friends, to the hottest place on earth.'

Fascinated by this strange and unexpected spectacle, nobody noticed that the wind had now died completely and an eerie silence had descended upon them. A few moments later, however, it was broken by a strange jingling noise. It sounded, for all the world, as though the sand was singing to them. To begin with it was distant, but very quickly it began to get nearer and grow louder.

'Look there!' Sir Alfred shouted suddenly, pointing into the sky beyond the pillars. 'What on earth is that?'

'Oh no!' Prince Omar cried. 'I don't believe it, it's a haboob.'

'A what?' Sir Luca asked with a look of horror on his face.

'A haboob,' Lord Balthazar replied. 'A terrible wall of burning sand. A wall that can reach thousands of feet into the sky. It's driven by the most ferocious wind and moves faster than the Golden Swift. It has the power to destroy everything in its path. It can uproot trees and flatten buildings, and I've heard of entire cities being destroyed in minutes. It'll be upon us in a moment. There's no escape. We must take cover behind one of the pillars and secure everything.'

Within moments, they'd hobbled the horses and laid them on the ground, staked the gear to the floor, and made sure the water was as safe as possible (they didn't want to end up like poor Mustapha). They tied themselves together by passing a long rope through their belts and lay over the horses' necks to try and prevent them from panicking. Then they waited.

They didn't have long to wait. The jingling noise soon became a terrible ringing. The sand was no longer singing; the entire desert was screaming at them. Then, suddenly, it was lost in a deafening roar as the wall of sand fell upon them. All light was extinguished, they were engulfed in total blackness and the heat became excruciating. They knew beyond a shadow of a doubt that without the protection of the pillar they'd have been swept to their deaths as easily as if they'd been rag dolls. But the pillar had withstood haboobs many times before, each encounter more damaging than the last. One day it would surely be toppled, but not just yet. It stood firm while the haboob swept past.

The terrible roar died down as quickly as it had come, and very soon another eerie stillness fell upon the desert.

'Is anyone hurt?' Lord Balthazar asked, climbing to his feet, brushing the sand and dust from his face.

Fortunately, the answer was no. Beyond a few minor burns and bruises, everyone had escaped unscathed. Their desert robes had done their job. It was difficult to know how long it had taken for the haboob to pass, but as the sand and dust began to settle the light returned and they agreed that they should press on till nightfall.

They made fast progress. The haboob had sucked so much sand from the desert floor that, provided they steered clear of troughs and valleys, they were walking over bare rock. The sand settled quickly but the dust that had been whipped up hung in the air, which meant they couldn't see too far into the distance. Through the haze they could see strange shapes: mysterious cities, castles and monsters, and hideous, malformed human faces. At first it frightened them but every time they drew close they could see the shapes were nothing more than rock formations that had been blasted and carved by the wind and sand.

As darkness began to descend they decided to set up camp for the night. They found a spot in the lea of a large rock which would protect them from any more winds from the north, and they hobbled the horses once more and passed a rope through their belts. As they sat round the fire dining on their meagre provisions, there was very little conversation. They were all exhausted, and one by one they fell asleep.

In the middle of the night a sudden bang woke them. Sir Alfred and Sir Luca leapt to their feet, swords drawn, ready to face an unseen enemy, but they were swiftly steadied by Prince Omar.

'Stand down, my friends,' he said. 'It's nothing but the cold.'

'What do you mean?' Sir Alfred asked.

'When night falls in the desert,' Prince Omar continued, 'the temperature drops dramatically. One minute the rocks are boiling hot, the next they're like a block of ice. It happens so quickly that they crack with a bang. We'll hear many more cracking rocks before the night is out.'

It was true, the terrible heat of the day had been replaced by a numbing cold.

'Are you sure it's not the work of djinns?' Sir Luca asked.

'I am, my friend. The djinns may well be responsible for many of the desert's mysteries, but they don't split rocks. It's simply nature. I suggest we all wrap up against this cold and try to get some sleep; tomorrow's going to be another difficult day.'

Apart from the cracking rocks, there were no more disturbances that night. Even so, no-one slept and as dawn began to break they were eager to continue their trek north and get away from this place as quickly as possible.

To begin with, the journey wasn't too difficult, despite their weariness. The ground below was still rock and there was no headwind, but it was unbearably hot. Although the dust from the haboob still lingered and blocked out the glare of the sun, its heat intensified as the day wore on and burned through their robes as it had done the day before. Every hour they had to stop for a moment's rest and a sip of water. By mid-afternoon their feet were badly blistered, and their dried lips began to crack. Prince Omar and the knights of Alcazar seemed able to bear this suffering, but Lord Balthazar became increasingly concerned that it was proving too much for the others. Princess Hannah started asking for water long before the hour was up and, twice, Sir Luca pointed excitedly to a lake of crystal-clear blue water in the distance, only to see it disappear as they drew nearer.

'It's called a mirage,' Prince Omar explained.

'Is it conjured up by the djinns to drive us all mad?' Sir Luca asked.

'No, like the cracking rocks, it's something that happens naturally in the desert. It's down to the heat and light.'

As the sun continued its journey west and beat down hotter than ever, Sir Luca appeared to have yet another vision.

'Look,' he shouted, 'a mountain.'

This time it didn't melt away. As they drew near they could see that it was real: a massive, steep-sided mountain that rose above the sea of sand and rock around it.

'Does this mean anything to you?' Lord Balthazar asked Prince Omar.

'It does, My Lord, it's the Giant's Shoulder. Legend has it that it's the petrified remains of the giant after whom this dreadful desert is named. It's said that one day, Ilderim, lord of the djinns, tried to pass through these lands but the giant refused passage. In his anger, Ilderim fought a terrible battle with the giant, swept his head from his shoulders and turned him to stone. That mountain is what's left of the giant.'

'I suppose that's why the mountain has no peak,' Princess Hannah said.

'Exactly, My Lady.'

'Does it give us any clues as to where we might be,' Lord Balthazar asked, 'or how much farther we have to go?'

'I'm not sure, My Lord,' Prince Omar replied, 'but if the giant tried to stop Ilderim as he was entering his domain, it may well be that we don't have too far to go.'

'Then let's press on,' Princess Hannah said. 'Let's try and get out of this desert before nightfall.'

Their minds might have been willing, but their bodies felt sore and worn out, and their progress was painfully slow. As dusk approached there was still no end in sight, and they decided to pitch camp and spend yet another night in the desert.

For Princess Hannah, it turned out to be the worst night of the entire journey. To begin with it was uneventful. After her companions had fallen asleep, she lay in the stillness watching the millions of stars twinkling through the veil of dust, thinking about her poor sister and wondering what might have happened to her. From time to time she felt as though she was drifting off to sleep but each time terrible visions brought her back to consciousness. Suddenly she sat up with a start. She could hear distant voices. Despite the bitter cold, she threw back her headscarf and listened. To begin with there was nothing, and after a time she decided it must have been her imagination playing tricks on her tired mind. But just as she was about to lie down again, she heard them once more, this time a little louder. She couldn't tell what they were saying; they sounded strange and alien, and after a moment they fell silent. Then she could hear shouting, as though someone was angry, and then a child crying. Suddenly Princess Hannah realised it was Fleur she could hear. She leapt to her feet, shouted to the others and ran towards the voices. The rope that tied them all together brought her to a sudden halt and dragged Prince Omar and knights to their feet, swords at the ready.

'What was it?' Sir Alfred shouted, helping her from the floor. 'What did you see?'

'It's not what I saw,' she said, 'it's what I heard.'

'What did you hear, My Lady?' Lord Balthazar asked.

'Listen,' she answered, 'can't you hear? It's Fleur. We've found her. She's crying.'

They all fell silent and listened. They could, indeed, hear what sounded very much like voices and a child crying.

'Where's it coming from?' Sir Luca asked.

'Over there,' Sir Alfred replied, pointing into the blackness.

'Let's take a look,' Lord Balthazar said. 'But step carefully and stay attached to this rope; we don't want to get split up.'

He held up a strange-looking orb which provided enough light for them to see a few paces ahead, and they stepped silently into the dark. With every step the voices got louder. One moment it sounded as though men were shouting, the next a child pleading and crying. Lord Balthazar exchanged glances with Princess Hannah. It must be Princess Fleur and her abductors, he thought, and he drew his sword. But just when it seemed they must be upon her, the voices stopped.

'Fleur,' Princess Hannah whispered, 'is that you? It's Hannah, can you hear me?'

There was no reply. Just silence. Then, a moment later, the crying started again, but this time it was coming from behind them.

Princess Hannah spun round and shouted, 'Is that you, Fleur? Tell me it's you. Say something.'

They rushed over to where they thought the voice had come from but, once more, it fell silent. It happened again and then again. Princess Hannah was dragging her companions in circles, as though they were chasing some will-o'-the-wisp.

'Enough!' Lord Balthazar said at last. 'It's not Fleur; it's the desert playing tricks on us again.'

That was the last thing Princess Hannah wanted to hear, but she knew Lord Balthazar was right and, as despair swept through her, she sank to her knees, buried her head in her hands and cried her heart out. It was too much to bear.

There were more ghostly voices that night. One moment they were singing and laughing, the next wailing and beckoning them all into the desert.

'Is that the desert playing more tricks?' Sir Luca asked. 'Or some evil djinn?'

'Who knows,' Prince Omar replied. 'Some say those voices are the spirits of dead travellers calling us to our deaths.'

The next morning they broke camp before dawn as usual and continued their journey north. They were now walking through soft sand rather than across the hard rock of yesterday, so progress was tiring and painfully slow, but easier on their blistered feet.

The dust that had hung over them since the haboob had now settled. The air had cleared, and visibility was good. When they stopped for a water break at mid-day they took stock of their surroundings. Looking back, they could see that, without realising, they'd been steadily climbing and, ahead of them, the desert continued to rise steeply towards a distant ridge.

'I think we've crossed the Giant's Shoulder,' Lord Balthazar said. 'The question is, what's beyond that ridge?'

As the incline grew steeper the climb became ever more difficult and by mid-afternoon they were having to zig-zag to avoid stumbling and falling back down the slope. They were especially careful to make sure the horses didn't slip. But as they neared the ridge there was more grass than sand underfoot and towards late afternoon they climbed over the ridge. Behind them a huge valley of rock and sand stretched as far to the south as they could see. On either side it was bounded by mighty mountain ranges: to the east the majestic sweep of the Flaming Mountains, to the west the steep forbidding slopes of the Snake's Back. Ahead of them was a vast plain, a sea of grass which swayed and rippled in the breeze from the north. To the west the peaks of the Snake's Back continued into the distance, to the east there was nothing but grass.

'So,' Sir Alfred said, once they'd recovered from the long, hard climb, 'this is where your map ended, Lord Balthazar.'

'It is, indeed. We're in uncharted waters now.'

'Do you think this is the creatures' land?' Princess Hannah asked.

'I don't know, My Lady, your guess is as good as mine.'

'So, which way do you think we should go?' Sir Luca asked.

'East,' Lord Balthazar replied, with a confidence he didn't really feel. 'To the west we've got the Snake's Back mountains, and to the north, if we can believe the legends, there's nothing but an icy wasteland. My guess is that the creatures have taken Princess Fleur east.'

'Then that's the way we must go,' Princess Hannah said. 'We've got several hours before dark. I suggest we make what progress we can on foot, rest the horses overnight and then continue on horseback at first light tomorrow.'

With that they left the ridge behind them and set off into the unknown once more.

7

THE HIGH PLAINS

To the great relief of everyone, the high plains were much cooler than the desert below. The sun was just as bright, but they were higher and there was a lovely fresh breeze from the north. It seemed to breathe new life into the horses, which, after their terrible struggle across the Giant's Shoulder, couldn't wait to stretch their legs on the grass. After an exhilarating gallop which quickly blew the dust from their lungs and sent the blood rushing through their veins once more, they settled into a steady canter.

There were very few signs of life on the plain. A frightened jack rabbit would scamper from under the horses' hooves from time to time, and Prince Omar spotted the occasional eagle riding the thermals high above. But as for any sign of man or creature, there was nothing until around mid-day, when Lord Balthazar called them to a halt.

'Look,' he said, pointing into the distance. 'Animals, it looks like goats.'

'And where there are goats,' Sir Alfred observed, 'there are usually men.'

'Or creatures,' Princess Hannah added.

'So, let's be on our guard,' Lord Balthazar replied.

They continued at a trot, and as they drew near they could see it was, indeed, a herd of goats, but as for a sign of any goat-herds, there was nothing.

'I would say that someone's spotted us and made themselves scarce,' Sir Alfred said.

'Should we look for them?' Sir Luca asked.

'No,' Lord Balthazar replied, 'it would be like looking for a needle in a haystack. I suggest we press on.'

Once they'd left the goats behind there were no further signs of life, and the hours passed by in monotonous silence until, suddenly, it was broken by Prince Omar.

'Look,' he shouted, 'to the north, riders, eight of them.'

'Can you make them out?' Lord Balthazar asked, straining his eyes in their direction.

'No, My Lord, they're too far away.'

'Do you want to approach them?' Sir Alfred asked.

'Yes,' Lord Balthazar replied. 'But with great caution, we don't know who they are. It could be a band of creatures. Whoever it is, we don't want to provoke an attack or frighten them off. Let's move towards them slowly and try to get a closer look.'

As they drew nearer they could see the riders had now stopped and were watching their every move. However, they showed no sign either of attacking or fleeing.

'They don't look like the creatures,' Sir Alfred said.

'Their skin isn't red and they don't appear to have any facial mutilations.'

'Can you see any weapons?' Lord Balthazar asked.

'They're carrying bows, My Lord, I can't see anything else.'

'No clubs?'

'No, My Lord.'

'Let's stop here,' Lord Balthazar said. 'I'm going to approach them alone, on foot.'

'Is that wise?' Prince Omar asked.

'I'm not sure, but we need to try and speak with them, so the less threatening we appear, the less likely it is they'll either attack us or flee.'

Lord Balthazar dismounted, made a point of laying his sword belt on the floor and began to walk slowly towards the riders. When he was about a hundred paces away two of them instructed their companions to canter away. Then they started to walk their horses slowly towards him.

'They're going to meet him,' Sir Alfred said to the others. 'Watch them carefully and let's be ready to move quickly if they start to look threatening.'

But there was no attack. It was difficult from a distance to see exactly what was happening, but it was clear that Lord Balthazar was succeeding in talking to these people. There was a lot of pointing, first at the other riders who'd just ridden off, and then in the direction of the Snake's Back Mountains and the east. It continued for some time and it appeared that Lord Balthazar was trying to explain where he'd come from and where he was heading. At last the conversation ended and the two horsemen cantered off to re-join their party.

'Did you find anything out?' Princess Hannah asked anxiously, as Lord Balthazar returned.

'A great deal, My Lady. Their language is similar to ours and it's not too difficult to understand them. They call themselves the Quiviri, and they say this is their land. They know the red-skinned creatures. They call them the Zhviek. They're from the lands to the north. A few days ago, two Zhviek turned up at one of the Quiviri villages to the east of here, seeking help for a sick child.'

'Did they say what the matter was?'

'They didn't know, My Lady, but they did say that the village is no more than a few hours away. If we ride fast we should get there before dark.'

'Can we trust these people?' Sir Alfred asked. 'Do you think they could they be sending us into a trap?'

'I don't know,' Lord Balthazar replied. 'We'll soon find out.'

They rode their horses as fast as they could, easing off only when they needed to catch their breath. The further east they travelled, the more they saw of the Quiviri. Most of them were travelling in what appeared to be small family bands like the one they'd just encountered, and all were heading west.

As the sun began to set beyond the Snake's Back Mountains, the village they were looking for came into view. It was a strange-looking settlement: a few white-washed stone houses with thatched roofs, ringed by a circle of round felt tents.

As they drew near six horsemen trotted towards them. Lord Balthazar called everyone to a halt, dismounted, laid down his sword and walked towards them just as he'd done a few hours ago. Again, his companions watched the conversation from afar, and again the Quiviri listened and seemed to understand. At length Lord Balthazar beckoned everyone forward and, escorted by the riders, they trotted to the edge of the village, where the Quiviri motioned them to stop. One dismounted and went into one of the tents while the others indicated that they should lay their swords and bows on the ground. Sir Alfred looked at Lord Balthazar uneasily.

'Do you think this is wise, My Lord?' he asked.

'We don't have a choice,' Lord Balthazar replied. 'If we want to speak with them, we must do as they ask.'

Reluctantly, they all laid down their arms and waited. After a few moments, they were beckoned into the tent. This was the moment of truth. Lord Balthazar stepped gingerly over the threshold, followed by his companions, all eyes peeled for any sign of danger. The tent consisted of a round stone fireplace surrounded by rough-looking cushions. It was illuminated by dimly burning wall torches and smelt strongly of stewed goat flesh.

One of the Quiviri was sat on the cushions on the far side of the tent, scrutinising his unexpected visitors intently and drumming his fingers nervously. A group of men armed with swords stood behind him looking on uneasily. The seated man invited his visitors to sit and motioned his men to close the door. That immediately prompted Sir Alfred to take stock of the situation and weigh his options in case things turned nasty. With the expert eye of an experienced warrior, he noted the layout of the tent and the strength and disposition of the Quiviri. He quickly concluded that they weren't warriors. Their swords looked old and blunt, and he guessed they'd never been drawn in anger. Most importantly they all looked frightened and he calculated that if it came to a fight, it wouldn't be too difficult to overpower them, even without weapons.

As soon as everyone was settled the man who was drumming his fingers cleared his throat and spoke. As Lord Balthazar had said, it was recognisable as their own language, though the accent was strange and horribly guttural.

'Who are you?' he asked. 'And where have you come from?'

'Sir,' Lord Balthazar replied, 'we're travellers from beyond the desert. My companions and I are from a land called the Golden Kingdom; our friends here are from the Kingdom of Alcazar.'

'Why have you come to our land?'

'We're looking for a child who was taken from our land by a band of Zhviek. We're here to find her and take her back.'

'How do we know that's true?'

'Because you know the girl passed through this village some days ago. The Zhviek brought her here and sought your help.'

'Who told you that?'

'A band of Quiviri travellers, out on the plain.'

The seated man turned to his companions and began what sounded like a heated discussion. At length he motioned his men to silence and turned back to his visitors.

'What you say is true,' he said. 'The Zhviek did bring a sick child to us. She was not Zhviek.'

'What was the matter with the child?' Princess Hannah asked.

'She was badly burnt by the sun and blistered. She was also sick with hunger and dehydration. Most of all she was exhausted.'

'Did you treat her?'

'Our women tended her injuries as best they could and gave her food and water, but the thing she needed more than anything was sleep, and that we couldn't give her.'

'Why not?' Princess Hannah asked.

'The Zhviek refused to leave her with us. As soon as the girl was fed they took her away.'

'Do you know where they took her?' Lord Balthazar asked.

'To the Black City.'

'How was the girl when they left?' Princess Hannah continued.

'She was ill. She needed rest. She could hardly stand.'

'How far are away is the Black City?' Lord Balthazar asked.

'A day's ride.'

Lord Balthazar exchanged glances with his companions and then turned back to the Quiviri.

'You've been most helpful,' he said, 'and we're very grateful. Now, with your permission, we'd like to leave immediately and make for the Black City without delay. We need to find the girl as soon as we can. Would you be able to provide some water and perhaps a little food for our journey?'

'You can't leave now,' the Quiviri said. 'You'll go in the morning.'

'May I ask why you don't want us to leave now?' Lord Balthazar asked.

'No. I've already said too much. You'll spend the night beyond the tents where my men can watch you. In the morning we'll return your horses and weapons and then you may go.'

'My Lord,' Princess Hannah whispered, leaning over to Lord Balthazar, 'we can't accept this. We need to get to Fleur as soon as we can.'

'I agree,' Sir Alfred added quietly. 'The knights and I can deal with these people.'

'No,' Lord Balthazar replied. 'We must accept. In two very short conversations with these people we've finally learned something about the creatures and where they're taking Princess Fleur. You can be sure we'll need their help again, so we've got to win their confidence, and we're not going to do that by leaving against their will or fighting our way out of here.'

Princess Hannah and Sir Alfred looked at each other and reluctantly accepted this reasoning. Lord Balthazar turned back to the Quiviri.

'We accept your generous offer, Sir. We'll be happy to sleep beyond the tents, but I must ask again if we may have some food and water?'

'We'll bring you water, but we have no food to share with you.'

'Thank you, Sir,' Lord Balthazar replied. 'May I ask you one more question?'

'What?'

'Can you tell us anything about the Zhviek?'

'No, I've said enough. My men will take you beyond the tents and bring water.'

'Well, I don't think much of the Quiviri,' Sir Alfred

said, as they sat beyond the tents eating what little was left of their supplies.

'Don't be too hasty to judge them,' Lord Balthazar replied. 'They're simple goat-herds. They've probably never seen strangers before and we've clearly frightened them. Now I suggest we all try to get some sleep. We're going to have another challenging day tomorrow.'

Princess Hannah couldn't sleep a wink after what she'd just heard; she was far too frightened for her sick sister, and as she lay gazing at the stars, she heard a single horseman gallop out of the village.

Lord Balthazar heard it too.

'It's a messenger,' he said. 'If I'm not mistaken, he's heading for the Black City with a warning. It's why we weren't allowed to leave. They're buying some time to prepare for us.'

The next morning, the man who'd acted as spokesman turned up with their horses and weapons.

'Ride east,' he said, 'towards the Dragon's Teeth and seek out the Altan-Quiviri. They will be expecting you. Now go.'

Once more they headed across the plains, stopping only to water and rest their horses. As the morning wore on they began to despair of ever seeing an end to the sea of grass and Sir Alfred wondered if they'd been sent on yet another wild goose chase. Then, around mid-day, a distant mountain range came into view and as they drew nearer they could make out the jagged peaks of what could only be the Dragon's Teeth mountains. From that point on, things began to look more promising. They passed a number of Quiviri bands, again heading west, and several villages, similar to the one they'd stayed at the night before. Towards the end of the afternoon, a much bigger village came into view, and riding from it, a large party of horsemen.

'Just as I thought,' Lord Balthazar said. 'We have a welcoming committee. Let's be careful, everyone.'

'This could be a little tricky,' Sir Alfred said quietly. 'They don't look any more like fighting men than the ones yesterday, but there are a lot more of them and they don't look so frightened.'

The Quiviri leading the pack rode up to Lord Balthazar and held up his hand in what appeared to be a greeting.

'Welcome to the land of the Altan-Quiviri,' he said. 'Follow me. My master wants to welcome you in person.'

Once again, they were taken to a tent on the outskirts of the village. From the outside, it looked like the one they'd been interrogated in the night before. Inside, however, it was very different. It was furnished with beautifully embroidered carpets and cushions and illuminated by fragrant candles. There was no stink of stewed goat meat.

They were greeted by a thickset man who was much more finely dressed than any of the Quiviri they'd seen so far. It also appeared he had some manners and, Sir Alfred noted, he was unarmed.

'My friends,' he said warmly, handing them over the threshold. 'Welcome to our land. Please make yourselves comfortable. You must be very weary from your travels.'

As they reclined on the luxurious cushions, he sat cross-legged before them.

'I am Altan, Chief of the Altan-Quiviri. I apologise for the bad manners you were shown by our people last night.

Unfortunately, we're not accustomed to strangers on these high plains and your unexpected arrival alarmed them.'

'Your people tried to help the child we're looking for,' Princess Hannah said, 'and for that we're very grateful. We understand the Zhviek have taken her to the Black City and that she's very sick. We need to find her as quickly as we can and get her back to her own land. Can you help us, My Lord? Can you take us to the city?'

'I'm afraid that's impossible,' Altan replied, 'at least for the moment. If you enter the Black City, you'll die.'

'What do you mean, My Lord?'

'The Black City is a place of great evil. Over the years, many people have entered, and most have died.'

'But if they've taken the girl there we must follow, whatever the risk,' Princess Hannah replied.

'Of course you must, but not alone. There are men among our people who are able to enter and return unharmed. They're called Blackfeet. I have taken the liberty of sending for one and I'm hoping he will be with us tomorrow. Until then there's nothing to be done. I insist you spend the evening here as my guests. I believe we have much to talk about.'

'My Lord,' Princess Hannah replied, 'we're very grateful for your kind offer of help and hospitality but we don't know you or your people. How do we know we can trust you? How do we know that you're not involved with the Zhviek?'

'You don't,' Altan replied, looking at her directly, 'any more than I can be sure I can trust you. But it seems to me that right now you don't have too many options. I suggest you accept my offer so that we can at least try and get to know each other. You never know, some trust may grow from that.'

'We do accept,' Lord Balthazar said. 'You're right. We're from different worlds and we have many questions for each other.'

'Excellent,' Altan replied. 'Now let us eat and drink a little and then we'll speak.' And at the snap of his fingers his men laid a mountain of food before his guests.

Altan could see they hadn't eaten properly for some time and he had the manners to leave them to their food, while he contented himself with a small morsel of meat and sat in silence watching them intently.

'My friends,' he said at last. 'There's one question which puzzles me above all others.'

His guests looked up from their food.

'What makes the girl you seek so important to the Zhviek that they would travel halfway across the world to seize her?'

'We've no idea,' Lord Balthazar replied. 'It's the very question we've asked ourselves a thousand times since she was seized. We don't know anything about the Zhviek and were rather hoping you might have the answer.'

'There must be something special about her,' Altan said pointedly.

'What do you mean, My Lord?' Princess Hannah asked.

'The Zhviek are nomads,' Altan continued, 'a simple people who prize their horses and goats more highly than their girls. I can't imagine what could have persuaded them to embark on an adventure such as this? As far as I'm aware no Zhviek has ever set foot beyond these plains before. And I'm also intrigued know why people like you would make such a long and dangerous journey across the burning desert to a world that's completely unknown to them for the sake of a single child. Surely you'll concede it all sounds a little implausible.'

Altan sat in silence for a few moments, peeling a piece of fruit, allowing his guests to digest his words. Then he continued.

'May I venture an explanation?' he asked.

'As you wish, My Lord,' Princess Hannah said. 'What is it?'

'I suggest, my friends, that the child you seek is no ordinary girl. As I've just said, the Zhviek don't cross the world to kidnap ordinary girls, any more than people with your bearing and manners risk their lives to bring them back.'

He then looked directly at Princess Hannah.

'I put it to you, my friend, that you're of noble blood, a princess, perhaps, and the girl you're looking for is your sister.'

Princess Hannah looked at Lord Balthazar and the others in astonishment.

'Don't be surprised, My Lady, your eyes can't hide the anxiety or pain you're feeling. When I told you that you couldn't go to the Black City tonight, your body bristled with anger and frustration. Now tell me, what are you holding from me? What's stopping you from telling me what's going on?'

Princess Hannah was about to respond but Lord Balthazar motioned her to silence and answered on her behalf.

'You're to be congratulated on your powers of observation and deduction, My Lord. We've underestimated you and I apologise for not being open with you. The simple truth is we don't know you or your people and we don't want to give anything away that might stop us from rescuing the child.'

'I understand, my friend, and I accept your apologies. And now we're past the games we can, perhaps, start to help each other?'

'Indeed, My Lord. My name is Balthazar. I'm first minister to the King of the Golden Kingdom, and this is Princess Hannah, his eldest daughter. My friend here is Prince Omar, son of the King of Alcazar, and these are our loyal knights. You're quite right, of course, the girl we seek is Princess Fleur, our King's second daughter. The fact that we're here in person is a measure of how important she is to us and our people.'

'Thank you,' Altan said. 'That explains who the girl is and why you're here, but it doesn't tell us why the Zhviek have taken her.'

'As I just said,' Lord Balthazar replied, 'it's a question we've pondered long and hard, but knowing nothing of the Zhviek, the only conclusion we can reach is that they intend to demand something from us in return for her release. In other words they intend to use her for some kind of negotiation.'

'Perhaps,' Altan replied doubtfully, 'but what could the Zhviek possibly want from you? As I've said, they value their horses and goats above their girls. I can't imagine what their motive might be.'

And he sat on the cushion, looking into the eyes of his guests once more, as if searching for an answer.

'Tell us what you know about the Zhviek,' Lord Balthazar said. 'Perhaps that will provide a clue.'

Altan considered the request for a moment, then took a long, deep breath and began.

'The Zhviek have been known to the Quiviri for centuries. They're nomads from the steppes beyond the Dragon's Teeth Mountains, a place we call the Shadowlands. They live in small clans and are forever on the move in search of fresh pasture for their horses, which they esteem above all things. It's said that they learn to ride before they can walk and devote their lives to caring for their herds. They shear and comb them to produce the felt they use for their clothes and tents, and horse meat is their favourite food, although they only eat it when their herds are numerous. At night they sleep in the saddle, guarding their animals against thieves and wolves. They can travel for days without food or water, surviving on their stallions' blood and their mares' milk. They hunt from the backs of their horses with eagles and Dragon Wolves. For that reason, they've never seen the need for the bow. Their preferred weapon is the club. For years we had no conflict with them. They would graze the lands to the north and we would keep to the south. From time to time there have been disputes over land, but nothing serious. Then, a few years ago, things began to change. We started getting reports of a change in the weather in the Shadowlands – winters getting colder and longer, and the Zhviek started bringing their animals further south onto Quiviri land. Three years ago, we had reports of the worst winter in living memory. Many clans lost their entire herds and, with them, their means of survival. In desperation they migrated south in far greater numbers than before and started stealing Quiviri animals and trying to take our land. Things settled down a little as the intense cold gave way to spring, and we began to tolerate each other once more, until about three months ago, when things began to get worse than ever.'

'What happened three months ago?' Lord Balthazar asked.

'The Zhviek started going into the Black City. Blackfeet reported seeing groups of them rummaging among the ruins as if they were looking for something.'

'I thought you said that people died if they went into the city,' Princess Hannah said.

'So, they do,' Altan replied, 'and that's exactly what started to happen to the Zhviek. But it didn't stop them. More and more began to come, and after a few weeks they started coming to the Quiviri villages outside the city walls. It appeared they were looking for things that had been taken from the city.'

'What things?' Lord Balthazar asked.

'Anything they could lay their hands on, artefacts and stones mostly.'

'What did they want with them?'

'I don't know. We speak little of their language, and they don't speak ours. To begin with their visits weren't too frequent. They were intrusive but not overly aggressive, but as I said to you, the Black City is a place of evil. Most people that go in get infected and die shortly after. Many Blackfeet have died over the years. We couldn't have the Zhviek coming among our people spreading evil and disease.'

'So, what did you do?'

'We started taking up arms and challenging them as soon as they approached, and for a time we contained them. It was the kind of stand-off we've had many times over the years. Then the Kara-Zhviek started coming to our villages.'

'Who are they?' Lord Balthazar asked.

'They're a sect that's risen from the disasters the Zhviek have suffered in the last few years. Many believe, as we do, that the Zhviek are descendants of the Anashi, the evil race who, in ancient times, built the Black City, from where they held sway over the high plains and lands beyond. Legend tells us that when that city was finally destroyed, not all the Anashi were killed. A few survived and fled beyond the Dragon's Teeth Mountains, where they became the Zhviek we know today. In their language, the word Zhviek means the ones that fled. The Kara-Zhviek believe that the disasters their people have suffered are of their own making, punishment for their weakness and acceptance of the nomadic way of life. They say that the time has come to re-claim their rightful place as a warrior race whose destiny is to rule the world once more. As a token of their dedication to that cause, and to make themselves as frightening and intimidating as they can, they shave and tattoo their heads and mutilate their faces. They slice their noses off leaving two open slits, they clip their ears into points, and cut away their upper lips to show teeth which they paint red and sharpen to points.'

'We've seen these creatures,' Sir Alfred said. 'It was they who took our Princess.'

'Then you know how monstrous they look,' Altan continued, 'and they've used that appearance to intimidate my people. The searches became more numerous and violent, and a number of villages were completely ransacked. Naturally, we sent men in to deal with them, but we found that while the normal Zhviek would back down and flee when confronted with armed men, the Kara-Zhviek would hold their ground and fight. The result was bloodshed and deaths on both sides. Men who once were prepared to make a stand against the ordinary Zhviek now began to yield to the Kara-Zhviek and take their families away. As you've already seen, many are heading west.'

'What happened then?' Sir Alfred asked.

'I think the Kara-Zhviek were emboldened by the sight of our people fleeing and they stepped up the raids even further. At the same time their tactics changed.'

'How?' Lord Balthazar asked.

'They seemed to lose interest in the artefacts and stones they'd been ransacking our villages for. Their attention turned to our women.'

'Your women?' Princess Hannah said. 'What did they want with your women?'

'We don't know. It started late one afternoon around two months ago. An unusually large raiding party attacked one of our villages in the north. The attack was directed by a strange-looking Zhviek. Without explanation they clubbed all the men to death, seized three women and rode straight back to the city.'

'What did you do?' Sir Alfred asked.

'As soon as we heard the news I called a grand council, a meeting of all the village chiefs, and we drafted a troop of mounted bowmen to patrol the land between our villages and the city.'

'Didn't you go after the three women?' Princess Hannah asked.

'No, it would have been too dangerous to take our men into the city, and even if we had, it's unlikely we'd have found them. We took the view that those three women were lost, and our focus should be on preventing anyone else from being taken.'

'Did the patrols work?' Prince Omar asked.

'Things went quiet for a few weeks,' Altan continued, 'but then the raids started again.'

'Did the Kara-Zhviek fight their way through your patrols?'

'No, the Zhviek have always been wary of our bowmen. They went round them. First, they attacked two more villages, one in the north and one in the south, and took another five women. Then, a few days later, we had word that a number of people fleeing west across the plains had been attacked and more women taken. That pattern continued for a few more days. Solitary bands attacked on the plains and women carried off to the Black City.'

'What do they want these women for?' Princess Hannah asked again.

'We've no idea,' Altan replied. 'It's always women of a certain age: between fifty and sixty. They show no interest in anyone younger or older.'

'Have you stepped up the patrols?' Sir Alfred asked.

'We've started getting people to travel in convoys, and we've recruited more volunteers to protect them. We hope that if people stay in large groups, protected by armed bowmen, it won't be so easy for the Kara-Zhviek to seize anyone.'

'Has it worked?'

'It seems to be working. There haven't been any more raids for a while now, either on the villages or on the open plains, and we've seen nothing more of the strange creature that had our men clubbed to death. They've not disappeared altogether, though. A number of raiding parties have been approaching our patrols between here and the city demanding we hand over the Blackfeet and anyone that's sick.'

'This gets stranger with every word,' Princess Hannah said. 'First they want artefacts and stones, then your women, and now they want the Blackfeet and the sick. Have you no idea what they're up to?'

'We've no idea at all,' Altan replied. 'Absolutely no idea.'

'Why do you say their leader's strange?' Lord Balthazar asked. 'What's strange about him?'

'Many things,' Altan replied. 'For a start, he's not a warrior. He's much too small and he's no horseman. He always rides pillion with someone else and has to be helped on and off the horse. His body's bent double and his limbs appear to be withered so he can't walk properly. He shuffles about like a sick river crab. It's difficult to be certain what he looks like because he always wears a cloak and hood, but people who've been close up say his skin is a horrible brownish-green colour, and full of open sores. They say he stinks like a dead fish. It seems he's had a few accidents in his time. Apart from all the cuts and scars he's got, he's missing an ear and a finger. Our people call him the Toad.'

Lord Balthazar's eyes suddenly twinkled. 'If he's not a warrior, who do you think he is?'

'We don't know. He's probably a shaman. He's clearly got authority over his men, and in Zhviek society it's only the greatest warriors or the shamans that hold the power.'

'Which finger's missing?'

'The little one on the right hand. Why do you ask?'

'Just curious,' Lord Balthazar replied, exchanging glances with Sir Alfred. 'What can you tell us about the disease people catch when they go to the Black City?'

'It's a disease of the mind,' Altan said. 'We don't know much about it, but we think there are three phases. During the first phase there's very little to see. There are no outward symptoms and it's not even clear that there's anything wrong. After about two weeks the victim enters the second phase. That's when their behaviour starts to change and even the gentlest and most polite person in the world begins to get unpleasant. This quickly progresses into uncontrollable anger and violence. That phase usually last about two months. In the final phase the victim loses control of themselves completely. They foam at the mouth, grind their teeth and thrash about with a terrible urge to kill. It puts so much pressure on their bodies that eventually their hearts burst. The end normally takes about two weeks. So, from start to finish it usually lasts about three months, though with some people it can be much longer. Why are you interested in the disease?'

'It could be important,' Lord Balthazar replied. 'Remind me, when was it that the Toad started taking your women?'

'About two months ago.'

'And when did he start asking for the Blackfeet?'

'About a month ago.'

Lord Balthazar took a sip of his drink, thought long and hard, and then looked into Altan's eyes.

'Are you sure the Toad's Zhviek?' he asked.

'Of course,' Altan replied, surprised by the question, 'what else could he be?'

'And are you certain he's male?'

'What on earth are you talking about, man?'

'I'm not sure,' Lord Balthazar replied, 'but perhaps the creature is neither Zhviek nor male.'

'What do you mean?'

'I've got a horrible feeling it could be someone we know, someone from the Golden Kingdom, a woman.'

'A woman? That's impossible!' Altan said. 'Women have no standing or importance in Zhviek society. A woman couldn't possibly lead a band of Kara-Zhviek.'

'But this is no ordinary woman,' Lord Balthazar replied. 'If my suspicions are correct, her name is Absinthia Blacknail and, you're quite right in one thing, Lord Altan, she is a shaman or, as we'd say, a witch.'

Lord Balthazar's companions were no less astonished than Altan.

'This sounds very far-fetched, My Lord?' Princess Hannah said.

'Indeed, it does, My Lady. But consider the facts: Lord Altan has just described somebody who is slowly recovering their human form, but still retains many vestiges of the toad she once was, hence the name she's been given. He's described someone whose body is still broken and corrupted by that terrible spell and the regeneration process, and somebody who bears the scars of her battle with Sir Alfred – the missing ear and little finger from the right hand. The description fits perfectly.'

'But what's she doing with the Zhviek?' Sir Alfred asked. 'And how could she have got here?'

'And what does she want with the stones, the women and the Blackfeet?' Princess Hannah added.

'I'm not sure,' Lord Balthazar replied. 'It could it be that Blacknail was collecting stones and artefacts because she believes they hold the key to the ancient magic. And it's quite possible that having found what she was looking for, the magic possessed her the way it possessed you when you came into contact with the brush in the catacombs.'

'But why did her attention suddenly shift from artefacts and stones to women?' Princess Hannah asked.

'Because her priority had suddenly switched from power to survival,' Lord Balthazar replied. 'She needed to find a cure for the disease that was beginning to possess her, and she still does.'

'But what's that got to do with the women?' Prince Omar asked.

'I suspect she's been conducting magical experiments on them, the way she experimented so cruelly on those poor creatures in the Emerald Forest,' Lord Balthazar replied. 'She's looking for a cure.'

'Could that explain why she's only interested in women of her own age?' Princess Hannah asked.

'I believe so, and I think that's why she became interested in the Blackfeet and the sick. She wants to study and experiment on people who've been in direct contact with the disease. Those like the Blackfeet, who've resisted it, and those who've succumbed to it. She wants to see how it develops and possesses people. She's looking for anything that might point to a cure.'

'But none of this answers Sir Alfred's questions,' Prince Omar said. 'If the Toad is this Blacknail woman, what's she doing with the Zhviek? And how did she get here?'

'I don't think it can be her,' Sir Alfred added. 'I don't see how she could have got here. Even if she did survive our encounter in the Emerald Forest and regenerate her human form she would have been much too weak to make the journey to these high plains. Her injuries were far too severe.'

'And how on earth could she have known about this place, anyway?' Sir Luca asked.

'These are all good questions,' Lord Balthazar replied, 'but let me ask another. Could it be that she was brought here?'

'What do you mean?' Sir Alfred asked. 'By whom?'

'By the Zhviek,' Lord Balthazar replied. 'We know that one band travelled beyond these lands to seize Princess Fleur. Could it be that others made a similar journey and found Blacknail? What do you think, Lord Altan? Is that possible?'

'I don't know,' Altan replied. 'As I said to you, the Zhviek are simple nomads who have never had any interest in the world beyond these plains. However, there is something that may be of interest. About two years ago a small Kara-Zhviek scouting party was sent into the Pass of Tears, one of the few passes that cut through the Snake's Back Mountains. I don't know who sent them or what their mission was, but I do know it failed miserably. A few days after they'd entered the pass, they came galloping back. Or at least some of them did. It seems they'd been ambushed by monsters. Apparently, they had the talons of eagles and the fangs of snakes and they tore a number of Zhviek limb from limb. Those who managed to ride back were swiftly put to death by their own people for failing in their mission, but not before they'd related how their leader had escaped the clutches of those creatures and managed to gallop to the other end of the pass.'

'Very interesting,' Lord Balthazar said. 'So, what do you think that the Zhviek would have done next? What would you have done in his position, Sir Alfred?'

'The creatures in the pass sound very much like Mist Elves,' Sir Alfred replied, 'in which case I'd get as far away from that valley as I possibly could.'

'What on earth are Mist Elves?' Altan asked.

'As the Zhviek related, they're dreadful creatures,' Lord Balthazar replied. 'They're a cross between a goblin and a snake. From the waist upwards, they're goblin-like, with long arms and huge claws. They have small heads with big round eyes, and powerful jaws and long fangs. Below the waist their bodies are snake-like. They live underground, in woody or rocky places, just like the Pass of Tears, and come to the surface to feed. They ambush their prey with a sudden, lightning-fast strike and drag them below ground to tear them apart. We sometimes come across them in the foothills of the Snowy Mountains and kill a few from time to time, but we've never managed to pull an entire body from the ground. We think they coil round roots and rocks and retract themselves. For that reason, we don't know very much about them.'

Lord Balthazar turned back to Sir Alfred.

'So, having escaped from that pass where would you have gone?'

'I couldn't say, My Lord, we don't know where the pass leads to.'

'Let's say it takes you somewhere near to the Ring of Fire.'

'The domain of the Fire Sprites,' Sir Alfred replied. 'Again, I'd try get as far away from those horrible little savages as I could.'

'Indeed,' Lord Balthazar said, 'as would anyone. So, fleeing from Mist Elves and Fire Sprites it's quite possible that our Zhviek found himself in the foothills of the Snowy Mountains. And it's conceivable that that's where he met Blacknail.'

'I understand that all this is possible,' Prince Omar said, 'and it's very interesting, but it's speculation; there's not a shred of evidence to support your hypothesis.'

'I agree,' Lord Balthazar replied, 'but let's imagine for a moment that Blacknail and the Zhviek did bump into each other. What do you think might have happened?'

'If it were me,' Sir Luca said, 'I'd have despatched that hideous witch without further ado.'

'And what would you have done then?' Lord Balthazar asked. 'How would you have set about getting home? You wouldn't have been too eager to try and get through that pass again and risk another encounter with the Mist Elves.'

'What's your point, My Lord?' Princess Hannah asked.

'My point is, that if this line of reasoning holds up, it's very likely that our Zhviek would have welcomed help from anyone. We know that Absinthia Blacknail is a wicked witch but in her weakened state it's unlikely that our Zhviek would have seen her as a threat. It's far more likely he'd have seen her as someone who knew this strange land and could, perhaps, guide him home by another route.'

'Blacknail wouldn't help anyone unless there was something in it for her,' Sir Alfred said.

'But perhaps there was something in it for her. Perhaps she saw in this Zhviek someone who could provide her with the protection she so desperately needed and, with his horse, a means of mobility? In other words, they both had something the other desperately needed.'

'That's all very well,' Altan said, 'but I fear you're overlooking one important fact. They speak different languages. They wouldn't have been able to communicate.'

'That would certainly have made things difficult, at least in the beginning, but it's an obstacle Blacknail may well have been able to overcome. You couldn't know this, Altan, but we're talking about someone who, several years ago, bent a dragon to her will.'

'These truly are fascinating theories,' Prince Omar said, 'but they're no more than that.'

'I agree, Your Highness, but I would ask you to bear with me just a little longer. Let's cast our minds back to last year's Grand Tournament. I'm sure you remember that strange knight who arrived out of the blue with his little hooded servant and demanded to enter the jousting contest.'

'How could we forget him?' Sir Alfred asked.

'Could it be that the knight was our Zhviek and his servant, Blacknail?'

'What makes you say that?' Sir Alfred asked.

'During the three days of the tournament something strange happened. Two attempts were made to break into the catacombs where Princess Hannah and her maid Polly had found the magic brush. At the time I tried to find out who was behind those attempts, but my investigations were entirely fruitless. And I certainly didn't associate them with the knight or his servant. But, given what we now know, I wonder if it could have been them?'

'But how could Blacknail have known about the catacombs, and why would she have wanted to get into them?' Princess Hannah asked.

'I'm not sure, My Lady,' Lord Balthazar replied. 'My guess is that on her travels through the Golden Kingdom and during her time at the tournament she heard about the magic brush and the Firestone.'

'From whom?' Sir Alfred asked. 'The whole affair was kept very quiet; only a few people knew about it.'

'You can't be sure of that,' Lord Balthazar replied. 'You're right, we did try to keep quiet the true nature of Princess Hannah's illness, but I fear that even the most loyal and devoted servants sometimes gossip and share secrets. Rumours spread quickly and easily in a place like the Golden Castle, and it's quite possible that Blacknail heard them and persuaded someone to tell her the full story, or at least some version of it.'

'I'm afraid you're losing me again,' Altan said. 'What's all this about a magic brush and a Firestone?'

'Forgive me,' Lord Balthazar replied. 'Let me explain. Some months before the tournament we're talking about, Princess Hannah discovered an ancient brush buried in the catacombs beneath our castle. It turned out that the brush was enchanted, and its magic possessed her the way the stones and artefacts from the Black City have possessed your people. Fortunately, our friends in Alcazar have a cure – the Firestone. Using the Firestone we were able to destroy the evil magic that was consuming Princess Hannah and nurse her back to health.'

'So, you think Blacknail tried to break into the catacombs to get her hands on the magic brush and the Firestone?' Princess Hannah asked.

'I think it's quite possible,' Lord Balthazar replied. 'If she did know about them, she wouldn't have been able to resist the temptation to get her hands on them.'

'But she failed,' Sir Alfred said. 'You said so yourself. Nobody got into the catacombs.'

'Quite so,' Lord Balthazar replied. 'But I don't think that's too important. The important thing is that as well as hearing about the magic brush and the Firestone she must also have had long conversations with her Zhviek about the City of the Dead, the Anashi and the terrible magic they brought into the world. She must have learnt that the legendary City of the Dead and the Black City are one and the same place, and that the Zhviek are descendent of the Anashi. It wouldn't have mattered that she couldn't get into the catacombs. She'd get her Zhviek to take her to the Black City, the real source of the power she craves.'

'But if that's true, why did the Zhviek waste time taking part in the tournament?' Sir Luca asked.

'Simply because of Blacknail's deep hatred of Sir Alfred,' Lord Balthazar replied. 'The opportunity to have her Zhviek kill him must have been irresistible.'

'So, what do you think happened then?' Princess Hannah asked.

'As we know, the Zhviek did try to kill Sir Alfred but he failed and as soon as the tournament was over he and his servant disappeared. My guess is that they crossed the Great East River and took the same route back to this place that we've just taken. And rather than being clubbed to death as a failure, this Zhviek was probably hailed for having brought the shaman who could unlock the secrets of the ancient magic and help the Kara-Zhviek recover their former greatness.'

'But what's all that got do with Fleur?' Princess Hannah asked. 'How is it going to help us find her?'

'If all these hypotheses are correct,' Lord Balthazar replied, 'it seems likely that Blacknail is possessed the way you once were, and she knows that the Firestone is her last hope. She must also know that neither Alcazar nor the Golden Kingdom would willingly allow her to get her hands on it, so the only thing she can do is to make us an offer we can't refuse. That's why she kidnapped Princess Fleur. She'll promise to kill her if we don't hand over the Firestone. She must believe that that's the only way she'll be able to persuade us to agree to her demand. I would guess that a ransom note was delivered as soon as the Zhviek had got Fleur was out of the Golden Kingdom. Blacknail must now be waiting for a response.'

'This is terrible,' Princess Hannah said, holding her head in her hands. 'We've no idea how either Alcazar or the Golden Kingdom have responded. What are we supposed to do now?'

'We need to act,' Prince Omar said. 'We're running out

of time. If Altan's correct, Blacknail's been possessed for about two months. We need to do something before she goes into the final phase, and the madness grips her. We can't afford to wait for any help from either Alcazar or the Golden Kingdom.'

'Prince Omar's right,' Lord Balthazar said. 'We need to act now. This is what I propose: as soon as our guide arrives tomorrow I'll go into the Black City and find Blacknail. I'll agree to go to Alcazar and fetch the Firestone provided she agrees to release Fleur.'

'Do you mean you're going to negotiate with her and hand over the Firestone?' Altan asked.

'Not for a moment,' Lord Balthazar replied. 'We could never trust her. She'd have us all killed the moment she got her hands on the Firestone. What I want to do is convince her that I am going to fetch it. If I succeed it should buy us enough time to hatch a plan to get Fleur out.'

'How can we be sure that Princess Fleur is still alive?' Altan said.

'We can't,' Lord Balthazar replied, 'but I believe she is, and I will not agree to anything until I've seen her.'

'What if Blacknail's already had a response to her demand? She'll know you're lying. You'll put Fleur in even greater danger,' Princess Hannah said.

'I don't think a message could have reached her yet. But anyway, it's a risk we've got to take.'

'What if Blacknail won't agree to let you see Fleur?' Princess Hannah asked.

'I'll tell her there's no deal. Either she lets me see Fleur or she can forget about the Firestone. But it won't come to that. She's not going to give up and let death take her now she's so close to getting her hands on the power she so desperately craves. Now, unless there are any more questions I suggest we get some sleep.'

'Before we retire,' Altan said, 'I have an observation to make: if all the things you've said are true there is much more at stake than the life of Princess Fleur. If this shaman survives and succeeds in mastering the ancient magic it will only be a matter of time before the dreams of the Kara-Zhviek are realised. They'll have the means to regain their power and rebuild their empire. After all these centuries they will once again be a threat not just to the people of these high plains, but to the whole world. Your own kingdoms will be in very great danger.'

'I think you're right,' Lord Balthazar replied. 'But you may rest assured, Altan, that I will not leave these high plains until Blacknail is dead. She has bitten us once too often. She will not do it again. As long as I live she will resurrect neither the evil magic nor the Anashi.

'Now, tomorrow is likely to be one of the most difficult days any of us have ever faced. I suggest we all get some sleep. We must be away long before dawn. I bid you all good night.'

8

THE THREE TOWERS

The Black City lay half a day's ride to the east of the Quiviri village, at the beginning of the vast plain which stretched between the Dragon's Teeth ridge to the north and the Flaming Mountains to the south. At this time of night, anyone looking over its ruins from the outer wall would have seen nothing but the three black towers of the citadel, silhouetted against the dark grey sky. Two of the towers, like the rest of the city, had long since fallen into ruin and now rose to no more than half their original stature, but the middle one remained standing to its full height, as if in defiance of the decay around it. And if the observer on the wall had looked carefully enough they would have seen a deathly pale, greenish-grey light flickering behind the windows at the very top of the tower.

The light came from a strange, green, jelly-like substance which bubbled gently in a wooden bowl that had been placed on a large table in the middle of the room. Every few moments the bubbling would rise to a crescendo and emit a puff of gas, before dying down to a gentle simmer again. The Quiviri called it Dragon Snot and many years ago it had been highly valued as a source of continual light which had made many a Blackfoot very rich. The problem was that every so often the gas would start reeking of rotting flesh, so the Quiviri started calling it Dragon Poo and it quickly fell out of fashion.

The room illuminated by the jelly was dark and dank with a cold stone floor and a high, vaulted ceiling. It was the shape of a pentagon. Four of the walls had huge windows which rose from floor to ceiling, but the fifth, facing east, was solid stone. An enormous wooden table had been pushed against it and was strewn with glass flasks and bottles of every shape and size, and a number of strange objects which looked like gruesome instruments of torture. On either side of the table there were four rusty iron cages each with a dying woman inside.

Apart from the desperate women in the cages there were two other people in the room. One was the witch, Absinthia Blacknail, the other was Ashgul, the Kara-Zhviek who'd brought her to these lands and introduced her to his people as the long-awaited shaman who would help them re-discover the long-lost magic of the Anashi. They were standing by the north-facing window, looking into the blackness towards the Dragon's Teeth Mountains, as if waiting for something to happen.

Blacknail was bent almost double, one hand on the wall at the side of the window, the other clutching her walking stick. She wore a filthy black cloak which reached down to her knees, but for once she'd thrown back the hood to expose a head which more closely resembled that of a newly hatched bird than a middle-aged woman. Apart from a few wisps of hair, she was completely bald, and it was clear that the regeneration process from toad back to human was far from complete. The skull had grown back to its former size, but the skin appeared to be lagging behind and was still so under-developed and thin that you could see the dark shape of her brain pulsating faintly within. In fact, the skin was stretched so tightly over the head that it was constantly tearing, so that rivulets of blood were forever trickling down her cheeks. Vestiges of the toad were still clearly visible, not just in the colour of the skin, but also in the numerous dark warts which still covered her neck and presumably the rest of her body. Her eyes, as black and wild as ever, were sunk deep in cavernous sockets and her mouth was largely toothless. Every few moments it would slacken as if the effort of keeping it closed became too great, and her tongue, long and hideous, would slip down her chin only for her to suck it back up with a vile slurping and slopping noise. The scars from her battle with Sir Alfred were still clearly visible. There was a gaping black hole where her right ear had once been, and the fist that gripped her stick was missing its little finger. Her arms and legs bore the marks of what must have been many a desperate struggle with the weasels and stoats of the forest in the days and weeks after the battle with Sir Alfred. But most disgusting of all were the pustules and sores which covered her body from head to toe and oozed a constant dribble of thick green pus. Not surprisingly she gave off the most vile smell imaginable.

If Blacknail was the epitome of nature perverted by evil, Ashgul was a picture of robust health and vigour. He had the dark reddish skin that was typical of his kind but was taller and more muscular than most. The front and sides of his head were shaven and tattooed in the Zhviek fashion, and at the back of his head his hair was gathered into a tight knot and an elaborate braid hung down his back. He had not undergone the facial mutilation of his peers. He had persuaded them that his sheer size, physical strength and piercing black eyes were far more intimidating than anything that could be carved by a knife. He was dressed in the Zhviek way, a short leather skirt and leggings, and he carried a knife at his waist, and a long, wooden-headed club was slung over his back. Ashgul had long believed that the Zhviek were descendants of the Anashi, and when the Kara-Zhviek began persuading people that their recent disasters were of their own making, punishment for their weakness and descent into the nomadic way of life, they found in him a passionate supporter. That passion, together with his physical presence, soon brought him to the attention of the sect's leaders who were eager to encourage him, and they selected him to lead the mission through the Pass of Tears. That mission was a complete failure but Ashgul convinced himself and the sect's leaders that it was the hand of fate that had miraculously delivered him from the clutches of the Mist Elves, and it was the spirit of the Anashi that had guided him to Blacknail. They had shown him his destiny. With the shaman's help, he would recover the magic of the Black City and Anashi power. And so it was that the leaders of the Kara-Zhviek gave him his second mission.

After a few moments' looking into the distance, the

wait was over. There was a sudden flash of lightning behind the mountains, followed by a deep rumble of thunder. The Black Storm was upon them. It happened every night. For the Quiviri it was simply a terrible storm that rolled in from the Shadowlands. For the Zhviek, and especially Ashgul, it was much more than that. It was the spirits of the Anashi returning to remind them of what they'd become and to demand the resurrection of their former glories. As the storm neared, a huge bank of cloud rose above the mountains and suddenly burst into a thousand white-hot forks of lightning which smashed against the jagged pinnacles of the mountain ridge, before descending on the forsaken, rain-drenched ruins of the Black City. With each crash of thunder the ground shuddered and the tower shook. But within moments it had passed, and the rain had stopped. Once more the moon and stars shone down on the shiny black basalt of the ruins, once again conjuring in Ashgul's mind an enticing image of what the city must once have looked like and what his destiny was.

'Now,' Blacknail said, interrupting his reverie, 'let's get those idiots in.'

Ashgul nodded and walked across the room to the heavy wooden door. He pulled it open and called the guards. A few moments later the two Zhviek who'd kidnapped Princess Fleur and brought her to the Black City were brought into the room.

'So, you allowed yourselves to be followed,' Blacknail said, glaring at them with her cruel, black eyes.

'No, Shaman,' one of them replied, completely surprised by her words. 'That couldn't be, we took every precaution possible. No-one followed us.'

'Oh, but they did. A whole group of strangers followed you. First to Endora's Pool, and then across the Giant's Shoulder and the plains, and eventually they joined up with their Quiviri friends. My spies have seen them with their own eyes.'

'No, Shaman, it must have been the others,' the creature protested. 'We followed your instructions to the letter. We did exactly as you asked.'

'It's not important whether it was you or your companions who gave the game away,' Blacknail replied. 'The simple truth is that as a team you failed, which means none of you can be trusted.'

As they noisily protested their innocence and tried to pull away from the restraining hands of the guards, Blacknail hobbled over to one of the windows and with a great effort heaved it open.

'Show them out,' she said.

With that the guards dragged their captives kicking and screaming to the window and flung them out, their bodies to be smashed and broken on the rocks below. Blacknail had a quick look down, grunted with satisfaction, then pushed the window to and dismissed the guards.

'Now,' she said, pointing to the table, 'let's get down to business.'

'Why did you kill them?' Ashgul asked, clearly angered by Blacknail's actions. 'They were trusted warriors who did exactly what you asked of them.'

'They didn't do what I asked of them,' she replied. 'They allowed themselves to be followed. Let me tell you something, Ashgul, if you truly aspire to resurrecting the power of the Anashi, and one day leading the Zhviek, you need your people to fear you. If they see you forgiving failure they won't fear you, and if they don't fear you they'll never follow you. They'll come to despise you. Don't you forget that, my friend, and don't lose sight of your destiny. Every action you take and every word you speak must serve it and be seen to serve it.'

With that rebuke ringing in his ears and the witch's black and evil eyes burning into him, he thought better of protesting further and leaned back in his chair.

'Now,' Blacknail continued, 'let's consider our position. We've got that Princess locked in the Tower of Sighs, and I assume the ransom note was delivered. It *was* delivered, wasn't it?' she asked, suddenly glaring at Ashgul.

'Of course it was,' he replied, annoyed that Blacknail doubted him. 'The moment we got the Princess to the grasslands a hand-picked team of Kara-Zhviek was sent to the Golden Castle with the note. Their instructions were to bring the girl's rescue party and the Firestone back here as quickly as possible. They should be here within days.'

'How do you know the strangers spotted by my spies aren't the rescue party?' Blacknail asked.

'It couldn't be them. They couldn't have got here by now.'

'So, who are they then?'

'I don't know. But they must be after the girl. Somehow, they must have picked up the kidnap party's trail and followed them here. I've no idea how they did that; the men chosen for the mission were masters of disguise and deception.'

'Perhaps they captured the decoys and got the information from them. Perhaps they tortured it out of them.'

'Both decoy teams knew they'd never return from that mission. They were happy to lay down their lives in the service of our cause. And I can assure you, they would not have caved in under torture.'

'Hmm,' Blacknail said, with a note of scepticism in her voice. 'I hope you're right. In any event we need to do two things. We need to make contact with these strangers as soon as we can and find out who they are and what they're up to, and we need to put extra guards on the girl. If they've come to try and free her we need to be ready. We need her for the ransom.'

'I'll make arrangements as soon as we're finished,' Ashgul replied.

'Good,' said Blacknail. 'Now let's move on. How's your condition?'

'It's worsening,' Ashgul replied with a sigh. 'As I told you before, it feels as though my head's in the grip of an iron fist. Each day it's tightening and as it does, it gets harder and harder to control my anger. You said my people would despise me if I showed signs of weakness. I'm more concerned that they'll despise me for my anger.'

Blacknail was about to answer when their conversation was suddenly interrupted by a loud and desperate wailing. It was coming from one of the women in the cages. She'd got to her feet and was banging her head against the bars.

'What's the matter with her?' Ashgul asked irritably.

'It's nothing,' Blacknail replied. 'It's one of the potions I gave her; it doesn't seem to be going down too well. Ignore her, it usually passes in a few moments. Now, have you got any other symptoms?'

But before Ashgul could answer there was another

outburst of wailing, this time much louder than the last. The poor woman was clearly in terrible pain.

'How long is this going to go on for?' he demanded, increasingly agitated by the noise. 'We can't hear ourselves speak.'

'As I just said,' Blacknail replied calmly, 'be patient, it usually passes in a few moments.'

'Let me have a look at her,' Ashgul replied, walking over to the cage.

What he saw horrified him. The woman's eyes were bulging dreadfully and looked about to pop out of their sockets. All her teeth had fallen out and her gaping mouth was swollen and bloody. Before she'd been seized by the Kara-Zhviek she'd been a picture of good health and, as one of the Quiviri Gentlewomen, the women who tended the sick and needy, she was a pillar of village life. Now, in the space of just a few days Blacknail had broken her in both body and spirit and reduced her to this wretched state. Dimly aware that Ashgul had approached her cage, she stopped beating her head against the bars for a moment and stared at him with a look of utter despair on her face.

'What on earth have you done to her?' Ashgul asked, turning back to Blacknail. 'I thought you were supposed to be curing these people, not killing them.'

'And so I am, but mastering the ancient magic was never going to be easy. Remember, it's been around for a thousand years, perhaps longer; it's not going to give up its secrets easily.'

'So, what exactly have you done to this creature?' Ashgul repeated.

'First I gave her the disease and once I was sure she was possessed I gave her a draught of Fire Water.'

'What's that?'

'You've seen it. It's the water from the font in the old temple.'

'You mean that freezing blue stuff that bubbles like boiling oil?'

'The very same,' Blacknail replied. 'I think it might be what I've been looking for. From what I've seen so far it appears to be doing something the ancient magic doesn't like.'

'Who've you tried it on, apart from this creature?'

'The last two groups of women you brought me.'

'But they all died,' Ashgul protested, 'every one of them, and it looks to me as though this one's going the same way. Look, Shaman,' he said angrily, 'it's no good finding something that kills the magic but kills the person as well. We need a proper cure, woman, a real cure.'

Ashgul turned back to the woman in the cage and as he did she let out a loud shriek, convulsed violently and showered his face with stinking, blood-streaked vomit.

Ashgul went wild. He threw himself at the cage, ripped the door from its hinges and grabbed the woman by the hair. He flung her across the floor and, towering over her, beat her with his club, again and again and again. At last he stopped and stood panting over her broken and lifeless body.

Blacknail watched in silence, waiting for Ashgul to calm down a little, and then said quietly, 'You'd better go and get cleaned up.'

He smashed his club down on the table and marched

out of the room. Blacknail waited until she was sure he was gone and then hobbled as quickly as she could to the other table at the back of the room. She rummaged through the old bottles, found the one she was looking for and took two long draughts of the brown liquid inside. Then she grabbed another bottle and two glasses, hobbled back to the table and sat down, staring at Ashgul's bloody club.

A few moments later he returned, cleaned up, but still shaking with anger and reeking of vomit.

'Sit down,' she said, pointing to the chair opposite. 'Have a drink of this, it'll calm you.' And she poured two glasses.

'After you,' he replied, taking one of the glasses but staring at it suspiciously.

Blacknail raised the other glass to her lips, threw her head back and swallowed its contents in one gulp. Satisfied that it wasn't poison, Ashgul did the same and felt a strange warmth course through his veins.

'Now,' Blacknail said, watching his every move. 'We were talking about your condition?'

'Let's talk about yours,' he replied irritably. 'What's happening to you?'

'The strangest thing,' she said. 'The magic appears to be possessing me as it does everyone, but in a rather different way. I think it's reversing the regeneration process. I'm beginning to turn back into a toad.'

'Then we really are running out of time,' he said. 'A toad's no good to me; you need to find a cure before it's too late.'

'I can't speed things up if you club to death the subjects of my experiments.'

Ashgul bristled and instinctively grabbed his club.

Blacknail glared at him again.

'If you use that on me,' she snarled, 'you'll kill the only hope you have. If I were you, I'd put it down and listen.'

Ashgul laid his club back down on the table and took another long draught from the bottle.

'Now,' Blacknail continued, 'as I was saying before we were so rudely interrupted, there are three parts to mastering the ancient magic. The first is to find a reliable and stable source that I can use to infect people, the second is to understand how the possession works, and the third is to find something with which to control or destroy it. So far, I've made good progress on the first two. I've found a number of artefacts which appear to act as hosts, and I'm beginning to understand how the magic's power is activated. But finding something to control it is proving much more difficult.'

Ashgul leaned forward and grabbed the bottle once more, but as he tried to raise it to his mouth he faltered and dropped it.

'What's the matter?' Blacknail asked, with a curious look on her face.

'I feel strange,' he said. 'Something's happening to me. I can't lift my arms. My body's going numb.'

'Interesting,' she replied.

She watched him for a few moments and then hobbled round the table. She lifted his limp arm and let it fall. She did it again with the other arm and then laid his right hand flat on the table.

'What are you doing?' Ashgul asked.

Blacknail didn't reply. She lifted the club and brought it down on his hand.

'Stop,' he screamed, staring wildly at his smashed and bloody fingers. 'What are you doing?'

'I'm just making sure,' she replied.

'Making sure of what?' he yelled.

Blacknail didn't answer. She smiled.

'You've poisoned me, haven't you?' Ashgul shouted, trying desperately to move his arms.

'Yes, I'm afraid I have. It's the juice of the Moon Fungus. It paralyses. As soon as it's worked its way through your body I'll finish you off properly.'

'But why?' Ashgul screamed with a panic-stricken look in his eyes. 'You need me as much as I need you.'

'That used to be the case,' Blacknail replied. 'But things have changed. The disease is possessing you much more quickly than I thought. You told me you're finding it ever more difficult to control your temper and I've just seen the results. Your behaviour is unpredictable and you're becoming more of a danger to me with every passing day. I simply can't sit back and wait for you to snap again and club me to death as you did that creature over there.'

'How did you do it?' Ashgul asked. 'How did you poison me? We drank from the same bottle.'

'Indeed, we did,' Blacknail replied. 'The answer's simple. I knew you wouldn't touch a drop until you'd seen me drink, so while you were gone cleaning yourself up I took an antidote. It's so powerful I could finish the entire bottle of poison without any effects.'

Ashgul groaned and tried desperately to recover some movement but the paralysis was spreading quickly. In a moment it had reached his voice and, slowly, it rendered him speechless. He lay back in the chair, defeated and as helpless as a baby, and waited for the inevitable. What a stupid and pathetic way to die, he thought.

'It's a great pity things should end like this,' Blacknail said. 'Apart from Red Fang, you've been the best friend I've ever had, and I'm sure you'd have realised your dream of ruling the Zhviek. Just think of the things we could have done together. You, a master of men, and me, the mistress of the most powerful magic ever known. We could have ruled the world.'

Blacknail rambled on until she was quite satisfied that the paralysis was complete. Then she pulled herself to her feet, hobbled back to the table by the wall and returned with a long, narrow-bladed knife. As Ashgul watched, absolutely horror-stricken, she touched the tip of the knife to his bare chest and pushed as hard as she could. She managed to get the blade halfway in but no matter how much she twisted and wiggled it, she didn't have the strength to get it in any further. As Ashgul heaved his chest and rolled his eyes, she hit on an idea. She lifted his heavy club and swung it against the butt of the knife. After three blows she finally managed to bury it to the hilt and sat back as a trickle of blood flowed from Ashgul's mouth and ran down his chest. When his head finally slumped forward and his chin fell to his chest she got up, went to the door and called the guards.

'Remove those bodies,' she commanded when the guards came in.

'What do you want us to do with them, Shaman?' one of them asked.

'Throw them through the window, after the other two,' she said.

And as the guards went to pick up the first body, that of the woman, Blacknail hobbled towards the window.

'Wait,' she said, stopping in her tracks. 'I've got a better idea. Take them down to the cellars and feed them to the Dragon Wolves. You take that one,' she said, pointing to the battered body on the floor, 'and you get the one at the table.'

As the first guard dragged the dead woman from the room the second went to the body at the table. He lifted the head and then fell back with shock.

'It's Ashgul,' he said. 'What's happened to him?'

'Never mind about him,' Blacknail replied contemptuously. 'The disease got too much for him. He decided to take his own life.'

'But he's not dead,' the guard replied. 'He's still breathing. He's rolling his eyes. It looks as if he's trying to say something.'

'Rubbish,' Blacknail replied, peering into Ashgul's stricken face. 'Death's upon him. He'll be gone in a moment. Now do as I command and feed him to the Dragon Wolves.'

'I can't do that, Shaman, he's our commander.'

Blacknail rounded on him. 'Now listen to me, Zhviek,' she hissed. 'Do exactly as I command, or I'll have you fed to the Dragon Wolves instead. Is that clear?'

The guard had seen far too much of Blacknail's ruthlessness and cruelty to doubt her word, and he submitted. Reluctantly, he dragged his master to the door.

'And when you've done that,' Blacknail shouted after him, 'send that captain of the guard to me. Tell him he's got a new job, he's just been promoted.'

Once the guard was out of the room, Blacknail slammed the heavy door shut and hobbled back to the table. The loss of Ashgul was unfortunate but not the end of the world. The Kara-Zhviek would find a replacement. What was much more worrying was her lack of progress in finding some way of controlling the magic that was possessing her. Time was quickly running out. If she couldn't come up with something soon it would be too late; she'd be halfway back to being a toad again. It seemed clearer than ever before that the Firestone was the key. She had to have it as soon as possible. Without it she would surely die.

*

While Blacknail pondered her dark predicament, Princess Fleur lay curled up on a damp and dirty pile of straw in the corner of her cell in the Tower of Sighs. Still wrapped in the torn and tattered potato sack she'd been thrust into in the classroom at Barnaby's Mill, she looked more like a wild animal than a King's daughter.

She couldn't remember much of the journey to this place. To begin with she'd been tied up in the sack and couldn't see a thing. Then her captors had forced some dreadful medicine down her throat which had made her so drowsy that she completely lost track of time. It was only when they got near to these black ruins that her head had begun to clear. Then she began to recall how she'd been pushed and dragged across scorching deserts and wind-swept plains. She remembered ghostly voices in the night, some kind and enticing, others scorning and mocking her. She remembered the vile food the creatures had forced her to eat, horrible greyish-brown strips of dried wood or leather that smelled dreadful. To begin with she simply wouldn't eat it, but when the creatures started prising her mouth open and stuffing it down her throat with their awful claw-like fingers, she gave in. The first few times she couldn't hold it down, but then the creatures would scoop up her vomit and push it back down her throat. Eventually, she became so terribly hungry that she forced herself to swallow it and keep it down. But the thing that came back to her most vividly was the terrible pain she felt from her sun-burnt face and terribly blistered feet.

She hadn't the faintest idea where she was, or why she'd been brought here. Her two captors had spoken often enough, usually to spit out instructions or scream at her in their hissing, snake-like language, but she hadn't a clue what they'd said or what they planned to do with her. All she knew was that they were the ugliest, smelliest and cruellest creatures anyone could imagine.

She wasn't sure how long she'd been in this cell and, to begin with, she hadn't even thought about trying to escape. She'd spent her time curled up shivering and sobbing, her hands clasped tightly over her ears to block out the hissing and spitting voices of the guards beyond the door. She thought of her mother and father and Hannah and wondered where they were and why they hadn't come to rescue her. At times she told herself they must be on their way and it was only a matter of time before they'd come banging the door down and her mother would take her into her arms and give her the biggest hug she'd ever had. At other times, she thought they must have given up searching for her. It was then that she began to wonder why she'd been brought here and what these creatures were going to do to her. She remembered the bedtime stories her father, the King, had told her about ogres and giants and witches and the dreadful things they sometimes did to the beautiful princesses they captured. Perhaps they were going to eat her.

Time and rest are great healers, and so too are thoughts of impending doom. Fleur decided that if no-one was coming to rescue her, she'd have to make her own escape. The night her captors had flung her into the cell it had been pitch black and she'd been absolutely terrified. She'd imagined all sorts of rats and snakes and other evil creatures lurking in its corners, and she'd quickly buried herself in the straw. But next morning there was a little light from the burning torch outside the door and from a narrow window in the wall high above her. It wasn't much but it was enough to make out that the cell was actually a round stone tower. There were no corners for her imagined creatures to lurk in. For a full-grown man or woman there wouldn't have been any way out. The window was too high to reach, and the door was locked and guarded every minute of the day and night. But her captors hadn't taken into account the cunning and determination of a seven-year-old princess whose elegant little fingers and toes could wriggle their way into the tiny gaps between the stones. Fleur's plan was to climb up the wall like a spider and escape through the window.

She lay on her patch of straw looking up at the narrow window, listening to the guards talking and squabbling. She was waiting for the thunderstorm. She knew that when that had been and gone the guards would sleep. As she looked through the window she could just about make out the moon and the black clouds scudding past it, and then she heard the distant rumble of thunder. Within minutes the full fury of the storm was upon them. The rain lashed and the lightning struck, and the whole tower shook. They were the most terrifying thunderstorms Fleur had ever experienced and for a fleeting moment she felt grateful that she was in the cell rather than outside. But that feeling passed with the storm, and as darkness and silence fell on the tower once more she crept over to the door to check on the guards. For a few moments they continued talking and then fell silent except for a loud, animal-like snoring.

Fleur went over to the wall directly below the window, easily found the gaps in the stones she wanted and began to climb. It was easier than she'd expected and the gaps seemed to grow wider and deeper the higher she went. Halfway up she stopped and looked back. She couldn't see the floor anymore, it had been swallowed by the blackness, but she could see the light from the torch through the grill in the door. It looked a long way down, much further than she'd imagined, and for a moment she felt queasy. But she took three deep breaths and continued to the window. At last, she hauled herself over the edge and sat for a while, gathering her strength.

The cell had now completely disappeared in the darkness. Outside it was not much better. There was a full moon, but it was mostly hidden by the dark clouds which followed on the tail of the storm. When at last the clouds thinned out and the light shone through, Fleur noticed two things she hadn't counted on. The rain had made the stones very slippy, and the tower appeared to be surrounded by a huge black lake. However, she wasn't going to turn back now, so she carefully pulled herself over the edge and began climbing down. She soon realised that this was much more dangerous than the climb up. It was difficult to find a good grip or see where to put her feet. Several times her toes slipped out of the cracks she found and only her fingers stopped her from falling. But she persevered and as she neared the floor it seemed the danger had passed. Had Fleur been an experienced rock climber she'd have known that the last few feet of a descent can be the most dangerous. Unfortunately, she wasn't, and in her eagerness to reach the floor she grew careless, lost her grip and fell into a thorn bush. The thorns went straight through the sack cloth and her clothes and pierced her in a hundred places. Within moments she could feel the blood flowing. But she didn't scream or even cry; she disentangled herself in silence and after a quick glance back at the window in the tower, to make sure no-one was watching, she crept down to the edge of the lake.

The water was black and choppy and stretched out as far as she could see. Fleur was a strong and confident swimmer. Like all the children in the Golden Castle, she'd had regular lessons since she'd been a toddler and had spent many a sunny afternoon swimming in the cool waters of Flamingo Lake. And during summer holidays, when her family exchanged the heat of the castle for the cool breeze of the Blue Palace, she'd spend all day and every day swimming and playing in the ocean. But this lake looked very different from either Flamingo Lake or the ocean.

She didn't know whether she was on an island or on a bit of land that jutted into the lake, so she began to walk along the shore to have a look. When the clouds obscured the moon, the world was plunged into total blackness and silence. From time to time she fancied she could hear something moving and was terrified that someone might be following her. But when the moon re-appeared there was nothing more sinister than the silhouette of the three towers. She cast her mind back to her journey to this place. Could she recall anything that might help her to escape and get back home? She vaguely remembered being dragged up and down narrow, winding streets and passages, past broken buildings. It had taken an age and there had been lots of stopping and angry arguments about which way to go. And then she remembered being pushed onto a boat. Did that mean she was on an island, rather than a headland? She'd no idea how long she'd been walking along this shore but, eventually, she could see the outline of ruins across the water. Were they the ones she'd been dragged through on her way here? Was that the way home? They looked a long way away, too far to swim, especially in this oily-looking water. What she needed was a boat. A little further along the shore, directly in front of the tallest tower, she found a broad bank of stone steps leading down to the water's edge. It looked a bit like one of the many wharves she'd seen on trips down the Great East River. Perhaps she'd find a boat there. She hurried down the steps and ran from one end of the wharf to the other, but to her great disappointment, she couldn't see any boats. She'd have to swim.

Gingerly, she dipped her toes into the water. It felt even colder than it looked. But there was no alternative, so she eased herself in. The cold took her breath away and as she pushed off, her hands were shaking and her teeth chattering.

She swam harder and faster than she'd ever done before and, as she settled into a steady stroke, she began to warm up. After a while she began to tire a little, so she turned onto her back and allowed herself to float for a few moments. She was encouraged to see that she'd already put some distance between herself and the island, but she didn't like the look of the pale light glowing behind one of the upper windows in the tallest tower. Frightened again that someone might see her, she quickly turned back onto her front and pushed on towards the far shore. It was then that she was seized by a terrible fear. Was there anything else in this lake? In her lessons at school, she'd heard about the huge octopuses and dreadful sea snakes that lived in the depths of the ocean. Did they live in lakes as well? She pushed her head below the surface and opened her eyes, but she couldn't see a thing. The world below was even blacker than the sky above, and probably went down and down without end. Her imagination began to run away with itself and she half expected a giant tentacle to come snaking out of the dark to grab her at any moment, or the dagger-like teeth of some sea monster to tear into her flesh. But at last she made it to the shore and, with a great effort, heaved herself up the steps. For a few moments she lay there, absolutely exhausted from her efforts, but as her strength began to return she realised it was far too dangerous to stay where she was. She had no idea who or what could be lurking in the shadows. For a moment she thought of running straight into the ruins and getting as far away from the island as she could, but they looked so black and ghostly she decided she'd wait for a little light. She crawled into a little alcove in a broken wall, pulled her soaking wet sack around her and fell asleep.

9

THE BLACK CITY

Thankfully, she didn't sleep for too long. Dawn was still some way off when she woke, and it looked as though nothing had stirred on the island. Turning back to the ruins, the first thing she noticed was how much they stank. It was a completely new smell to her and she had no idea what it was. Perhaps, it was the smell of dead people and rotting bodies, she thought.

Despite her fears about going into the ruins, she knew it would be too dangerous to stay where she was. As soon as the guards realised she was gone they'd be after her, perhaps with those dreadful animals she's heard howling and snarling in the night. So, taking a deep breath, she plunged in. She couldn't see much of the streets and alleys she crept along because of the dark, but when the moonlight allowed, she could make out ruined buildings on either side. They were silent and black, but not blind. Fleur suddenly had the terrible feeling that her every step was being watched. By whom or what she didn't know, but something told her she wasn't alone. Despite the risk of making too much noise or bumping into something terrible, she decided to run as fast as she could. It was difficult. The streets and alleys were as twisty as she remembered, and sometimes they narrowed into nothing more than passageways. In no time at all she was out of breath, as much from fear as from the running, and she rested a moment, leaning against an old doorway. Suddenly she heard something moving inside and she quickly jumped back. Her first instinct was to run from that door as fast as she could, but something strange was stopping her. She couldn't say why, but she felt as though she was being drawn into the building. Almost against her will, she crept back to the door and peered inside. It was black and silent and just when she thought she must have imagined it, there was another movement. Then she heard a voice whispering to her, begging her to come inside. She was too terrified to do anything. Her legs felt as though they'd turned to jelly and she could neither run nor go in. The thing inside asked her again and again to go in, and she sensed it was getting angry. Then there was a sudden flurry of movement and two horrible amber eyes appeared out of the blackness, the cruellest eyes she'd ever seen. It broke the spell, her legs came back to life and she charged blindly up the nearest alley as fast as her legs would carry her.

It wasn't long before she was completely out of breath again. She felt as though the stones and everything else in this evil place was sucking her life away. She fell against a wall and looked back to see if those vile eyes were following her. Mercifully, they weren't, but something very odd had happened. The passage she'd just fled along had completely disappeared. Where it should have been, there was nothing but a solid, black wall.

Once she'd recovered her breath she walked back to the wall and, very gingerly, stretched out her hand to touch it. She half expected it to open up and reveal the passage she'd just run from, but it didn't. It was solid stone, like any other wall. This was impossible, she thought, and she turned to look at the rest of the street. It was long and narrow and black, just like all the other streets in this dreadful place. On either side there were buildings with windows. Most were broken, or crumbling, and some were still intact but covered in centuries of grime. She started walking very nervously towards the other end of the street, taking care to stay in the middle and as far away from the windows as she could. But as she neared the far end, it began to narrow, and soon, if she stretched out her arms, she could almost touch each side. And then she had another shock which stopped her in her tracks. There were people behind the windows, watching her. They were still and silent, and draped in tattered rags, the remnants of what must once have been clothes. Their skin was dry like ancient parchment, their eyes had long since dried to nothing, leaving empty black sockets, and their lips had tightened, revealing long yellow teeth. They looked as though they'd been dead for hundreds, perhaps thousands, of years and Fleur shuddered. She'd have given anything to be able to close her eyes as tightly as she could and banish those horrible faces from her mind. But she couldn't. She felt the same strange urge to go towards them that she'd felt in the doorway a few moments ago. As the end of the road approached, the urge to go closer became overwhelming and, leaning towards one of the windows, she peered inside. One of the figures looked like a girl of about seven, her own age. She wiped the grime from the window to have a better look. The girl was dressed in rags like all the others, her skin was dried and parchment-like, and her eyes had long since disappeared. But suddenly, just as Fleur was about to turn away, two eyed appeared in the sockets. Evil-looking, amber eyes, like the ones she'd just seen. And as they fixed her with a dreadful stare, the mouth opened and let out a hideous burst of laughter. And then they all started laughing, on both sides of the street and all around her. Fleur screamed in horror and fled up the street, as far away as she could get. She didn't stop until the street had broadened into what looked like a broken-down square. As she ran across it towards one of the corners leading out, she tripped on a broken cobble, went sprawling on the floor and banged her knee. Instead of jumping straight up, she grabbed her knee, pulled it to her chest and curled into a ball. Then she lay crying. This place was too much to bear.

When, at last, she opened her eyes she was surprised and hugely relieved to see that dawn had broken. The sun was rising in the east and the shadows were beginning to retreat. She prayed that the evil eyes and fiendish cackling would go with them. The ruins around her looked every bit as horrible as they had in the dark but, somehow, they didn't seem quite so frightening. The square was only small and was surrounded on each side by the usual fallen-down buildings with their ghostly windows but, mercifully, she couldn't see any signs of life behind them. There was nothing but stillness and silence. Then suddenly she knew she was being watched. She leapt to her feet and stared into the windows. There was nothing: the figures from the night were gone. But suddenly the silence was broken by more laughter. This time it wasn't the laughter of the dead; it was a big, black raven perched on one of the broken walls. As soon as she saw it, Fleur knew instinctively that this wasn't any old raven; it was watching her with a purpose. After a while it opened its broad black beak and laughed again. More ravens quickly answered the call and settled on the ruins around it. And then more and more came until a whole conspiracy had gathered. To begin with they simply watched her in silence. Then they all started laughing and cackling together. At last, one of them took to the sky, circled the square three times and flew off towards the rising sun. Fleur knew its destination. It was heading for the three towers to alert the guards.

In a pique of anger, she leapt to her feet and ran towards the remaining ravens, waving her arms and screaming at them as loud as she could. With a flurry of feathers they were gone, leaving her screams to echo round the square, but in a very strange way. The first echo was so quiet she could hardly hear it, but the following ones grew louder and louder until they were ringing in her ears. Then, suddenly, they stopped, and silence returned. Fleur sat and wondered how on earth an echo could get louder and louder rather than quieter and quieter as they did at home. As she pondered this she noticed something else that was weird: the shadows. Instead of running away from the sun, they ran back to it. Everything seemed to be either upside down or inside out. It wasn't only the most horrible and frightening place she'd ever been to, it was also the strangest and most sinister. Suddenly her musings were interrupted by a terrible premonition that someone or something was hunting her, and she was gripped by an irresistible urge to get as far away as she possibly could.

*

While Fleur had been making her escape from the clutches of Blacknail and the Kara-Zhviek, Princess Hannah and the rescue party had been galloping across the plain towards the Black City. They arrived just after dawn, and Altan took them straight to the north-west turret, the highest point on the ruined battlements, from where there was a good view of the entire city. The Blackfoot who'd agreed to take Lord Balthazar into the city was due to arrive in a few hours. In the meantime, Altan introduced them to a man called Vasco who'd been a Blackfoot many years ago and was said to know more about the Black City than anyone else.

'It's much bigger than I imagined,' Lord Balthazar's said, as he took the view in.

'And it used to be much bigger than this,' Vasco replied. 'The original city stretched further to the east and it's said that when the Anashi empire was at its height, it took two days to walk from one end to the other. But when they were finally defeated it was completely destroyed and the survivors fled to the island you see in the distance. There, they build a smaller but more heavily fortified city, protected by the lake and high walls. The walls have long since disappeared, but you can still see the three towers. As the Anashi gradually recovered from defeat, the city spread and grew back to the size you see now.'

'Have you any idea where my sister's being kept prisoner?' Princess Hannah asked.

'I can't be certain,' Vasco replied, 'but she's probably being held in one of those towers on the island.'

'And do you know where we'll find Blacknail?' Lord Balthazar asked.

'Who's Blacknail?' Vasco asked.

'The Toad, it's a she, do you know where she's likely to be?'

'My guess is that you'll find her and her Kara-Zhviek friends in the tallest tower, and I think the girl will be in the smaller one behind it, the Tower of Sighs.'

Princess Hannah and Lord Balthazar strained their eyes towards the towers.

'From here, it looks as though it shouldn't be too difficult to get to the island,' Princess Hannah said.

'You're quite right,' Vasco replied. 'From here it looks as though it should be easy. But once you're in those black ruins, things start to look very different.'

'Is there a map of the city?' Lord Balthazar asked.

'A map wouldn't do you any good,' Vasco replied. 'Nothing remains the same in this city; everything changes from one day to next. Buildings that were in one place yesterday are no longer there today; they've either moved or disappeared completely. Paths that led you to one destination, now take you to another, and doors that were open are now closed.'

'Have you seen that with your own eyes?' Princess Hannah asked, incredulously.

'Many times,' Vasco replied. 'And that's not all. Shadows point towards the sun rather than away from it, and echoes grow louder instead of fading. Water spins clockwise one day, and anti-clockwise the next. In some places fires burn with the intensity of the blacksmith's forge; in others they freeze everything around them. There are black spots where lightning strikes from a clear blue sky. On some days a heavy stillness and silence hangs over the place; on others the ground trembles and shakes.'

'Have you any idea what's behind these phenomena?' Lord Balthazar asked.

'The evil magic created by the Anashi. Following defeat, their hatred of everyone and everything grew stronger and stronger and they became obsessed with revenge. All their energies went into finding a truly evil magic with which to destroy the people who'd defeated them and driven them away. They almost succeeded. Somehow, they managed to conjure up and unleash the most powerful magic the world has ever known, but they weren't able to master it. Instead it began to destroy them and the few that survived fled beyond the Dragon's Teeth Mountains. From then on, the deserted city became a battleground between nature and evil. To begin with evil had the upper hand, and chaos reigned, followed by stagnation and decay. The whole place was de-stabilised, and the laws of nature, as we know them, ceased to apply. But nature fought back and slowly the tables are turning. Each day evil's grip on this place is being loosened. One day it will be gone completely, and the laws of nature will prevail again. Flowers will grow once more, and people will re-claim this land as their own. But that is still a long way off. For now, the evil magic remains, and it is still potent and very dangerous.'

'If a map's no good, is there anything else we can rely on to guide us across the city?' Lord Balthazar asked.

'Yes,' Vasco replied. 'The Blackfoot's ability to read the signs. As I said a moment ago, the whole place is in a constant state of flux, things change from day to day, so experience counts for nothing. You need to understand what the signs are telling you. On some days you get the feeling that nature's guiding you, protecting you; on others you sense that evil is trying to lure you to oblivion. That's why you need a Blackfoot. For anyone that can't read the signs, the city's a death trap. Either they disappear, never to be seen again, or they return possessed, and die a horrible and lingering death.'

'Are there any living creatures amid the ruins,' Princess Hannah asked, 'any people?'

'The only creature to make its home among these ruins is the raven. That's why they're shunned by our people and worshipped by the Zhviek. Apart from the ravens, there's nothing, not even rats or insects. Even the trees and plants shrivelled and died centuries ago. As for people, I don't know. There are countless tales of eerie voices and mysterious shadows lurking in the dark, but if you ask me, they're nothing but tall tales. There's no life as we know it, but the ruins are far from dead.'

'Do you ever go into the city?' Sir Alfred asked, clearly fascinated by all this.

'I've not been beyond these battlements for years,' Vasco replied. 'There was a time when I'd go treasure hunting several times a week. I prided myself on being able to read the signs and even started to believe that nature was protecting me. I became complacent and careless, and one day took my ten-year-old son with me. We had a great trip, one of my best ever, and we returned with a huge bag of weird and wonderful artefacts which we sold for lots of money. But nature hadn't protected my son. To my horror, we soon discovered that he'd been possessed by the magic. It took three long months for him to die. But even then, I didn't learn my lesson. A while later I ventured back only to suffer the accident that crushed my legs. Now I can't go anywhere without these sticks. I couldn't go back into that place even if I wanted to.'

For a while Lord Balthazar, Princess Hannah and the others continued to quiz Vasco about the Black City and his fascinating and frightening experiences as a Blackfoot, when suddenly Prince Omar, who'd climbed to the very top of the tower, called out.

'Look,' he said, pointing into the distance, 'I can see something.'

They all turned to where he was pointing. To begin with they couldn't see anything but then, sure enough, they could see a small brown and red figure darting between the ruins.

'It's my sister,' Princess Hannah cried out with a thrill of excitement. 'It's Fleur.'

'And she's coming towards us,' Sir Alfred added.

'My Lord,' Princess Hannah said, 'I have to go to her.'

But just as she was about to jump down the steps, Lord Balthazar grabbed her arm.

'Forgive me, My Lady, but I can't allow you to do that. You heard what Vasco said: to go into the city without a Blackfoot would be certain death.'

'Then what do you want me to do?' she shouted in

exasperation. 'Just sit here and watch? I can't do that, My Lord.'

'You must, My Lady, you must be patient a little longer. You've already been possessed by this evil once; who knows what would happen if it struck you again. Remember, we don't have the Firestone with us. We must wait for the Blackfoot. As soon as he gets here I'll go in and get her.'

Princess Hannah pulled herself from Lord Balthazar's grip and turned back to the ruins.

'Where is she now?' she cried, suddenly panic-stricken. 'I can't see her anymore.'

'It's alright,' Prince Omar said. 'She's still there. She keeps disappearing behind broken walls and fallen-down buildings, but she's still there.'

'Where's that Blackfoot?' Princess Hannah asked Altan. 'Shouldn't he be with us by now?'

'Yes, he should. He's late. I don't know what's happened. I'll send men to look for him.'

Within moments four riders were galloping from the tower, back towards the Quiviri village. On the battlements all eyes were trained on the ruins, desperately trying to keep track of Fleur.

Princess Hannah felt sick. She was straining her eyes so hard they felt as though they were about to pop out of her head. Her mouth was as dry as a bone, and her heart was beating like a drum. When Fleur disappeared from view she broke into a cold sweat; when she re-appeared she felt faint with relief.

'Something's following her,' she shouted, pointing behind her sister. 'There's a shadow, it's gaining on her.'

Everyone looked to see what it was.

'I can't see anything,' Sir Alfred replied. 'It's your imagination, it's playing nasty tricks on you.'

'There is something over there, though,' Lord Balthazar said, pointing to the island.

'What is it?' Princess Hannah asked, anxiously.

'I'm not sure, there seems to be some sort of commotion.'

'It's boats,' Prince Omar said. 'They're landing and a number of Zhviek are getting out. They're running up and down the shore.'

'They must have discovered that Princess Fleur's escaped,' Altan said.

'Can you make out what they're doing?' Lord Balthazar asked, squinting his eyes as hard as he could.

'I'm not sure,' Prince Omar said. 'It looks as though someone's taking charge. He's called them together and appears to be giving orders.'

'And what happening over there?' Sir Luca asked, pointing a little further along the shore.

'It's more Zhviek,' Prince Omar said. 'And they've got six huge black dogs with them.'

'They're not dogs,' Altan said. 'They're Dragon Wolves.'

'They're what?' Princess Hannah asked, in horror.

'They're wolves from the Shadowlands; the Zhviek use them for hunting.'

'You mean they're going to set wolves on my sister?'

'I'm afraid so, and two of the Zhviek have eagles.'

'What are they for?' Sir Alfred asked.

'They use them to locate their prey and direct the Dragon Wolves to the kill.'

'This is absolutely dreadful,' Princess Hannah shouted.

'We have to do something. If we wait any longer those wolves will tear my sister to pieces.'

'Can you still see Fleur?' Lord Balthazar called to Prince Omar.

'Yes, My Lord. She's still making her way towards us.'

'Is anything happening on the shore?'

'The Zhviek are fanning out, but they don't seem to be doing anything.'

'They're frightened of the city,' Altan said. 'They don't want to enter it.'

While the Zhviek were messing about on the shore, Fleur continued her flight through the ruins.

'If those Zhviek don't sort themselves out soon,' Prince Omar said, 'Fleur's going to be alright. She's going to make it.'

But the Zhviek did sort themselves out. Another boat pulled up and two evil-looking Kara-Zhviek leapt out. They started laying into their men with long black whips, and within seconds the Zhviek were all tearing through the ruins. Then the eagles were released and the hunt was on. But at the very moment Fleur needed to run harder and faster than she'd ever done before, she faltered and sank to her knees against a wall.

'What's happened?' Princess Hannah asked, as she watched the situation take this horrible turn for the worse.

'It must be fatigue,' Lord Balthazar replied. 'The poor child looks exhausted.'

'My Lord, please do something, those beasts are hunting my little sister.'

'Is there any word of the Blackfoot?' Lord Balthazar asked Altan.

'Nothing, My Lord, no-one can find him.'

Princess Hannah looked at Lord Balthazar, pleading with him to do something.

'She's up, My Lady,' Sir Luca said excitedly, 'she's on her feet and she's started running again.'

'She's going the wrong way,' Prince Omar shouted in alarm. 'She's heading straight to the Zhviek.'

'My Lord,' Princess Hannah said. 'I'm begging you. Do something, now, please.'

'What's that?' Sir Alfred said, pointing to the sky.

'It's the eagles,' Altan replied.

For a few moments they circled over the ruins and then started screeching.

'They've spotted her,' Altan said. 'They're signalling her position to the Zhviek. In a moment they'll release the Dragon Wolves.'

Lord Balthazar realised it was only a matter of time before they'd catch Fleur and that he couldn't wait a moment longer.

'I'm going after her,' he shouted. 'No-one is to follow me, is that understood?'

As everyone nodded their agreement he leapt from the wall with an agility that amazed them all and ran into the City of the Dead.

*

Fleur heard the howling of the Dragon Wolves the moment they were released and knew immediately that she was being hunted. She sensed that she was running in the wrong direction and abruptly turned back the way she'd come. She was completely out of breath now, her legs were turning to jelly again and her heart was beating like a kettledrum. But she refused to give in. She might only be small and seven, but she wasn't just any girl: she was a king's daughter, and she would fight like one. She could hardly see now. Tears and sweat were blinding her, and the howling was getting nearer and nearer. She drove on and on, and quickly turned to look behind her. Disaster struck. She stumbled, her legs gave way and she fell heavily on her back. She tried desperately to scramble back to her feet, but it was too late. A huge black Dragon Wolf with yellow fangs and a lolling red tongue came bounding towards her and leapt for the kill. Fleur covered her face in absolute horror and waited for the end. But it never landed. There was a huge bang, a blinding flash of light and the animal was smashed against the far wall. As it fell to the floor in a crumpled, stinking heap, two powerful arms swept Fleur off the floor and, once again, she was careering away from her pursuers.

But the howling didn't stop. It grew louder and louder. Her rescuer was strong and fast, but he wasn't as fast as the Dragon Wolves. Slowly but surely, they were closing on them. Suddenly he turned down a narrow side alley and through a broken gateway into a walled courtyard. He bounded to the far wall searching desperately for a way out, but disaster struck again. There was no way out. They'd reached a dead end. They were trapped. Her rescuer backed up against the wall and sat Fleur down against it.

'Don't you worry,' he said gently. 'We'll soon have you out of here.'

Fleur looked up into his face and burst into a flood of

tears. It was Lord Balthazar. They *had* come to save her, after all, she thought. Overcome with a mixture of fear and exhaustion, she collapsed back against the wall. She was no longer quite sure what was happening; everything was beginning to go hazy. But she did notice one thing: there was something different about Lord Balthazar, something she'd never seen before. His eyes were twinkling, as they always did, but not with their usual kindness and good humour. This time they were glowing with martial fury.

The Dragon Wolves came charging through the gateway but pulled up abruptly when they saw their prey was trapped. They prowled back and forth, snarling, salivating and staring, waiting for the order to kill. After a few moments, a shadow passed over the courtyard as the eagles landed. They perched on one of the walls, fixed their evil eyes on their prey and, like the Dragon Wolves, waited. For a few moments a deathly silence hung over the place, until the Zhviek filed noisily through the gateway. Lord Balthazar made sure he was shielding Fleur as best he could and turned to face the creatures, staff in one hand, sword in the other. Fleur took one last look, covered her eyes and curled into a tight ball. This was it, she thought, the end.

Then, behind them, there was a voice.

'First the wolves attack,' it said, 'and then the eagles grab their prey. I've seen it done before. It works every time.'

'Who's that?' Lord Balthazar demanded, without taking his eyes from the foe in front of him.

'It's the Blackfoot,' the voice said. 'Apologies for getting here a little late, I'll explain later. Move slightly to your left behind that pile of rubble and do exactly as I say. I can get the little princess out of here if you can buy me a little time. Can you do that?'

'How much time do you need?' Lord Balthazar asked.

'Just enough to put those beasts off while I get her through this gap in the wall. Is there anything you can do to distract them?'

'I can give them some fire to play with,' Lord Balthazar replied. 'Tell me when you're ready.'

He could hear something moving behind the wall. It sounded like heavy boulders moving against each other. In front of him, one of the Kara-Zhvick appeared through the gateway. An evil grin contorted its hideous face as it took in the scene. They'd got the girl back. It looked at the Dragon Wolves and the Zhviek, raised its huge whip and was just about to crack it when there was a cry of 'Now!' from behind the wall. Lord Balthazar swung his staff and hurled a massive ball of flame at the Zhviek and their dragon wolves. It exploded with an enormous bang and, as the beasts recoiled from the heat and flame, he and Fleur made their escape. They slipped behind the rubble and squeezed through the narrowest of gaps in the wall. Once through, the Blackfoot pulled a lever and a huge boulder rolled forward to seal the gap.

'Now run,' he said, and hurtled off down a dark narrow passage.

Lord Balthazar swept Fleur into his arms once more and set off after the Blackfoot. The tunnel was long and dark and went up and down, but the floor was even and their way was illuminated by bowls of greenish-grey light. At last they could see daylight at the end of the tunnel and in moments were back in the open. To Lord Balthazar's huge relief, the passageway had brought them back to the battlements. He ran across two hundred paces of open ground as quickly as he could, and in a few moments was back with his companions.

Princess Hannah leapt down the stairs, swept Fleur in her arms and, with tears of joy streaming down her cheeks, gave her the biggest hug imaginable.

Altan cut the welcome short. 'Listen,' he shouted, 'the Dragon Wolves are coming.'

And sure enough, the howling was getting nearer and nearer.

'Let me take Fleur,' Lord Balthazar said to Princess Hannah. 'As you can see, she's collapsed. I need to tend to her and make sure she's alright. The most useful thing you can do right now, is to take your bow against those wolves.'

The last thing Princess Hannah wanted to do was let go of her sister, but she knew Balthazar was right. He was the physician and could do far more for Fleur than she could. So, she, Altan and the Quiviri bowmen took up positions on the tower and along the battlements while the knights mounted their horses and rode out onto the open ground beyond the walls.

A few moments later the Dragon Wolves were upon them, followed by the Zhviek, who were still being thrashed by the whip-cracking Kara-Zhviek. The two sides then weighed each other up across the wasteland.

'Listen to me,' Sir Alfred shouted, making sure the archers above could hear him as well as the knights. 'If I'm not mistaken, the wolves will lead the attack, so I want you, Princess Hannah and the archers, to focus on them. I need you to take them out, to kill every last one. Is that clear?'

The archers shouted their agreement.

'Knights,' he continued. 'Once the wolves are dead, the Zhviek will attack. We must stand firm until they're halfway across the wasteland. At that point Sir Luca and I will advance to engage them. We'll drive through them, taking as many as we can, and wheel round at the far wall. As soon as we're done it's your turn, Silver Riders. I want you to ride through them, cutting down as many as you can. When you reach Sir Luca and me, we'll make the return journey, skewering as many more of them as we can, and then it's back to you. It shouldn't take more than a few passes to get the job done. If I'm not mistaken, there's not going to be much fight in these cowardly monsters.'

The Zhviek did exactly as Sir Alfred had anticipated. With blood-curdling howls, the Dragon Wolves hurtled towards them. The ground shook under their weight and the knights had to work to steady their frightened horses.

On the battlements, Princess Hannah carefully took aim and loosed one of her golden arrows. As true as ever, she hit her target. The arrow pierced the black beast between its yellow eyes and sent it rolling into the dust. That gave the Quiviri bowmen the confidence they needed and, together, they loosed a hail of arrows. Some missed their target but many struck home. They brought the wolves to an abrupt halt and knocked some of them over, but they didn't kill them. The Quiviri bows weren't as powerful as Princess Hannah's, and their arrows weren't as heavy. Princess Hannah instructed them all to fire at the nearest beast while she dealt with the others. Three more golden arrows hit their mark in quick succession and three more beasts fell dead. But the last one was not giving up without a fight. It had been struck with so many arrows that it looked more like a hedgehog than a wolf, but it wouldn't give up. Princess Hannah marked a target between those evil yellow eyes once more and loosed her last arrow. With a final howl, the beast fell bleeding in the dust.

Now it was the turn of the Zhviek, and with a few more loud cracks of the whip they too came charging down on the knights, screaming and shouting, and whirling their heavy clubs.

The knights waited and waited and then, on Sir Alfred's command, he and Sir Luca charged to engage them. In moments they were galloping at full speed and as soon as they were a few paces away they lowered their lances, marked their targets and charged through the onrushing mob. As they turned round at the far wall they could see that two of the Zhviek were lying dead. The Silver Riders began their attack and the Zhviek stopped in their tracks at the sight of the dreadful, curved scimitars poised to cut them down, but it didn't do them any good and six more of their number were quickly despatched. This wasn't a battle, Sir Alfred thought, it was a slaughter. He'd been right: there was no fight in these creatures. He expected the big Kara-Zhviek to show a bit more spirit but was disappointed. Rather than standing and dying an honourable death, they tried to run back to the passageway leading out of the courtyard. Unfortunately for them one of the Silver Riders blocked the way and took their heads.

With the battle over, Princess Hannah ran back to her sister and was quickly joined by the other archers and the knights.

'How is she?' she asked.

'She's sleeping,' Lord Balthazar said. 'I've given her a draught of medicine. I think she's going to be alright, but she's exhausted and needs rest more than anything.'

'The Zhviek and the Dragon Wolves are dead,' Sir Alfred said. 'What's the plan now, My Lord?'

'We need to get Fleur to Alcazar as quickly as we can. There's every chance she's been possessed by the evil magic, so we need to get her to the Firestone. You must all head for the desert right away. Altan and his men will provide an escort, and you'll be given food and fresh horses along the way.'

'Do you think the Zhviek will follow?' Sir Alfred asked.

'I've no idea,' Lord Balthazar replied. 'We don't know what they're going to do.'

'What about you, My Lord?' Princess Hannah asked. 'Aren't you coming with us?'

'Later,' he replied. 'But first I have unfinished business to attend. Hopefully it won't take too long, and when I'm done I'll catch up with you in the desert. Then it's a question of finding our way across the Giant's Shoulder and through to the other side. Assuming we succeed, the carpeteers will be waiting for us and then it's all back to Alcazar. Now go, everyone, before the Zhviek come back.'

He watched them all mount up and set off towards the Quiviri village. Then he exchanged a last wave with Princess Hannah and headed back to the City of the Dead.

10

ALCAZAR

The return journey across the Giant's Shoulder was much easier than the first crossing. The mysterious forms that shimmered in the haze, and the voices that called in the night, were just as frightening as before, but everyone was ready for them this time. Most importantly, there was no haboob to contend with, and to everyone's huge relief, Lord Balthazar caught up with them just before the avenue of pillars. Shortly after that they were back with the carpeteers.

As soon as they reached Alcazar, Fleur was taken into the care of Lord Zubin and his medical team. For the first few days she slept but gradually the combination of rest and medicine had the desired effect, and she began to recover her strength. In no time at all she was up and about and eating properly.

Princess Leila, Omar's sister, was desperate to help

Fleur's recovery as much as she could. She and Princess Hannah had been best friends since they were children and had spent many summers together, so she knew Fleur well and knew that she loved nothing more than dressing up. So, as soon as Lord Zubin said it was alright, she asked Sabrina, the dressmaker, to show Fleur some of her latest creations. Of course, Sabrina was only too happy and she decided to put on a real show.

As show time approached the three princesses took their seats on a huge divan piled high with beautiful soft pillows. Fleur looked much better than when she'd arrived. Lord Zubin's lotions and potions had quickly worked their magic on her blisters and bruises, and a succession of luxuriously perfumed bubble baths had helped her feel like a princess once more. The filthy clothes she'd been wearing when she arrived, and that horrible potato sack, had been consigned to the fire and replaced with a beautiful new silk dress, as light and delicate as a butterfly's wing.

Sabrina's show was fabulous. Her dresses weren't only beautiful, they were magical, and as she and her assistants swirled and twirled around the room, they shimmered and sparkled, and the ancient legend of the dressmaker came to life before their eyes. Sabrina told Fleur she'd make her any dress she wanted. All she had to do was choose. Fleur smiled graciously and said they were all so beautiful she couldn't decide. But her eyes still looked tired, her smile was forced, and after a while she leaned back on the cushions and began to suck her thumb.

Princess Leila could see that the show wasn't having the effect they'd hoped for and was relieved when Lords Balthazar and Zubin came into the room.

'I can see we're missing something quite spectacular,' Lord Balthazar said enthusiastically. 'Would you mind terribly if we interrupted for a moment?'

'Not at all, My Lord,' Princess Leila answered, 'we were just about to finish, anyway.'

Lord Balthazar knelt down in front of Fleur and gently took her hands in his.

'Now then, my little princess, how are you enjoying the show?'

'They're beautiful dresses, My Lord,' Fleur replied.

'Have seen a special one, one you'd like Sabrina to make for you?'

'Not yet.'

'And how are you feeling today? How are your burns and blisters?'

'Everything's getting better, I think, but I'm still very tired.'

'Of course you are,' Lord Balthazar replied. 'That's only to be expected. Why don't you have a little rest this afternoon, just for a while?'

'I know,' Princess Leila said, 'would you like me to tell you a story? The one about Zina and the djinn, perhaps?

Fleur nodded.

'Come on then, let's go and find a nice shaded spot by the turquoise pool.'

As soon as they'd left the room, Princess Hannah turned to Lords Balthazar and Zubin.

'How is Fleur?' she said. 'Is she alright? Her burns and bruises seem to be healing, but she's not herself. She's quiet and withdrawn. Is that normal?'

'It's only to be expected, My Lady,' Lord Balthazar

replied. 'Physically, she's doing very well. As you know, we were very concerned that she might have been possessed by the evil magic while she was in the City of the Dead so, as soon as we arrived here, Lord Zubin laid on the Firestone. Contrary to our expectations there was no reaction at all, and to be doubly sure we laid it on a second time. Again, there was no reaction, so we're pretty sure she's escaped unscathed. Fleur is young and strong and she's reacting well to the treatments Lord Zubin has prescribed, so there's every reason to believe she'll be as good as new in no time at all.'

'However,' Lord Zubin added, 'her mind may take a little longer to repair. We must not forget how terrifying this experience has been for her. One moment she was happy and carefree in the company of her friends, the next she was seized by the most frightening-looking creatures I've ever heard of. She was blindfolded, drugged and then carried off to a dark dungeon in an unknown land. It's hard to imagine what she must have thought was happening. It would have been too much for many a knight of the Companions or a Silver Rider, let alone a seven-year-old child.'

'Do you think it's damaged her mind?' Princess Hannah asked, clearly worried by Lord Zubin's words.

'Almost certainly,' Lord Zubin replied, 'but I'm absolutely confident that with the right treatment and lots of love and care, she'll make a full recovery.'

'Can you make her forget what she's been through?' Princess Hannah asked.

'No, My Lady, that would never work, and it's not what we're trying to do. What we want to do is deal with the fear and pain associated with her experiences. We started work the moment she was up and about, and, already, there's evidence it's working. Our hope is that in time, when Fleur thinks about these experiences, it will be like reading a book. The things that happened will all seem real, but it will feel as though they happened to someone else, one of the characters in the book. And it will be that character, not the real Fleur, who feels the fear and pain.'

'You say, in time, My Lord: how long do you think the treatment will take?'

'It's difficult to be sure, My Lady, but, as Lord Balthazar's just said, Fleur is extraordinarily strong and resilient. You must expect her to be withdrawn for some time, weeks, perhaps, but that is part of the healing process. Her mind is trying to make sense of everything that's happened. Gradually, she'll start putting the experiences in one compartment and the fears and pains in another. And the treatment we're giving her will help to speed up that process and help to lock the fears away.'

'Is there anything I can do?' Princess Hannah asked.

'Continue as you're doing now. Asking Sabrina to put on a show was exactly the right thing to do, even though it didn't work out as you and Leila wanted. I'm absolutely certain that the real Fleur will soon be with us again. Just be patient and give her time.'

As Princess Hannah and the two wise men continued their conversation about Fleur's health, Princess Leila returned with Sir Alfred and Prince Omar.

'Is Fleur sleeping now?' Lord Balthazar asked.

'Yes, My Lord,' Princess Leila replied. 'I told her two stories, but she fell asleep halfway through the second, so

I've put her to bed and asked the maids to stay with her.'

'And how is the poor child doing?' Prince Omar asked Lord Zubin. 'How well is she recovering?'

'She's doing very well,' Lord Zubin replied. 'As I was just saying to Princess Hannah, what she needs more than anything is rest and a little time.'

'I'm relieved to hear that,' Prince Omar said. 'And I know she couldn't be in better hands. Now, let me order some cool lemonade and perhaps Lord Balthazar would tell us what happened when he returned to the City of the Dead.'

'I'd be happy to, Your Highness,' Lord Balthazar replied, and as soon as the lemonade arrived, he began.

'I can safely say that the City of the Dead is the most dreadful place I've ever been to. For the first time in my life I have smelt the odour of evil and I pray it will be the last time. It is also the strangest place. Without the Blackfoot I'd probably still be in there, going round and round in circles. But he was an excellent guide. He was pretty sure we'd find Blacknail at the top of the tallest of the three towers in the Citadel, and he proved to be right. I expected a Kara-Zhviek reception committee when we got there, but there was nobody and I was able to go up unchallenged. The sight that awaited me was dismal. Blacknail was sitting alone at a large table in the middle of a dark, damp room that reeked of death and decay. She recognised me straight away and asked if I had the Firestone. When I told her I hadn't, she thought for a moment and then hauled herself up and hobbled over to one of the windows. She told me she knew Fleur had escaped and that her team of Zhviek were all dead. She looked down on the ruins and fell silent.

I got the impression she was weighing up her predicament. After a few moments she seemed to have made a decision and turned to me. Her time had come, she said, and she asked me to help her put an end to her life. I was only too ready to oblige, and a short while later she was dead.'

'How did you kill her?' Sir Alfred asked.

'With her own poison,' Lord Balthazar replied.

'Were any Kara-Zhviek still there?' Prince Omar asked.

'No,' Lord Balthazar replied, 'the Blackfoot and I searched all three towers and the rest of the citadel. There were plenty of signs of recent activity, some of it very gruesome, but all the Zhviek and their Dragon Wolves had gone. The place was completely deserted.'

'Have you any idea where they went?' Prince Omar asked.

'No, Your Highness, they appear to have either left the city or melted into the stones.'

'Well at least we can rejoice in Blacknail's final demise,' Sir Alfred said.

'I'm not sure we should rejoice in any part of Blacknail's story,' Lord Balthazar replied. 'It's a desperately sad story, and one which reflects very badly on the Golden Kingdom.'

'Why is that, My Lord?' Princess Hannah asked. 'You never told us the story. What happened to Blacknail?'

'I don't remember all the details, My Lady, I wasn't involved until it was too late, but this is what I do recall: Absinthia Blacknail was an only child. Her family were chocolate farmers. They lived in a pretty village called Cloud View, in the foothills of the Snowy Mountains. Everything about the family was normal and respectable. At school Absinthia proved herself to be a clever girl, but she was shy and aloof and, because of that, not very popular with the other girls. She preferred her own company and that of the ladies of the hedge, the ladies who seek out herbs and spices for medicines. From them she developed a love of nature and an understanding of the importance of careful observation, and she started keeping a diary in which she recorded her thoughts and observations.

'As she got a little older the other girls began to resent her aloofness and started to bully her. To begin with it didn't seem to worry her too much, but one day one of the girls stole her diary and read out some of the entries. They included observations of her classmates as well as of nature. From that point the bullying got worse. Then, suddenly, the girls who were most vocal in their bullying began to suffer minor illnesses and ailments. The question of poisoning arose and the finger of suspicion was pointed at Absinthia. Things deteriorated quickly and the class teacher and parents got involved. However, things weren't handled well, and the whole village started to turn against Absinthia's mother and father as well as the child. It was all too much for Absinthia's mother and, quite suddenly, she died. That devastated Absinthia and I think it's at that point that we lost her.

'After her mother's death the bullying stopped for a while, but a few months later one of the girls said something especially nasty and within days she'd died a very painful death. Once again the finger of suspicion was pointed at Absinthia. This time people felt the evidence against her was overwhelming and they decided to bring her before the village elders. But she had other ideas. Rather than try to defend herself in the face of such hostility she fled to the hills. Efforts to find her and bring her to account continued for months and then years but to no avail. Then things took another sinister turn for the worse. A dragon began to attack the search parties and then Cloud View and all the other nearby villages. Houses were destroyed, villagers killed, and a number of children were seized and swept away to the hills, some said to be devoured. There was no longer any doubt in people's minds that it was all Absinthia's doing, and Lords Lupus and Aguila both sent armed search parties into the mountains. But they couldn't find either Absinthia or the dragon. The reign of terror continued unabated until, eventually, Sir Alfred here took the dragon's head and laid it at the King's feet. I believe that was the act that triggered Absinthia's final descent into madness. From then on it appears that all her energies and considerable intelligence were channelled into revenge. Sir Alfred and the entire kingdom were now her prime targets. She would do anything to hurt them and I think we all know the rest.'

'A sad story, indeed,' Princess Hannah said. 'My sister might never have been put through this ordeal had the bullying been dealt with properly.'

'And I wouldn't have been half killed in the Emerald Forest,' Sir Alfred added.

'What do you and Lord Zubin propose to do about the Zhviek and the ancient magic?' Prince Omar asked.

'I'm not sure we need to do anything about the Zhviek,' Lord Balthazar replied, 'at least for the time being. Before re-joining you in the desert, I had a lengthy conversation with Altan. He seems to think they won't be a problem now that Blacknail is dead. As you know, the Quiviri and the Zhviek have lived alongside each other for centuries and although there have been occasional conflicts, for most of the time they manage to co-exist. He's not asking for any help on that count and believes that interference from outside might upset the balance and natural order of things.'

'But what about the Kara-Zhviek?' Prince Omar continued.

'That's a rather different question.' Lord Balthazar replied. 'It seems to me that the key question is whether this dreadful cult can survive the deaths of its shaman and most able captain. Perhaps without them it will lose its impetus and fizzle out. But if it does survive and start to re-invigorate itself, Altan may well need our help. And that raises another question: would either of our kingdoms want to get embroiled in the affairs of these people?

'Lord Zubin and I will be discussing all these issues with the Council of the Wise and we'll present our conclusions and recommendations to the two Kings. It will be they who make the final decisions.'

'What about the evil magic?' Princess Hannah asked.

'That's the biggest question of all,' Lord Zubin replied. 'If the Kara-Zhviek were to find a way of mastering it they would acquire enormous power and become a great threat to the peoples of these high plains and perhaps beyond. The Zhviek would re-emerge as the new Anashi. We could never allow that happen. We would need to stop them.'

'Do you think the Kara-Zhviek *could* master the magic?' Prince Omar asked.

'I don't know,' Lord Zubin replied. 'The little we know about them suggests it's unlikely. We don't know how many times they've tried before but whatever they've done they don't appear to have got very far.'

'Do you think Blacknail got anywhere?' Sir Alfred asked.

'We'll never know,' Lord Zubin continued, 'but we do know that she didn't get far enough to find a way of protecting or curing herself from its deadly effects. In the end she realised she needed the Firestone.'

'If we ever did need to act,' Princess Hannah asked, 'what would we do?'

'We might need to think about seeking out the Guest People,' Lord Balthazar said. 'It's they who created the Firestone and, as far as we know, they're the only ones who have any real understanding of the evil magic.'

'Who are the Guest People?' Sir Luca asked.

'I think it's best if Lord Zubin answers that,' Lord Balthazar replied. 'He knows far more about them than I do.'

'But nowhere near as much as I'd like,' Lord Zubin said. 'I believe that in the Golden Kingdom they're known as the Wanderers. Many years ago it appears they came into contact with the evil magic of the Anashi and it caused them terrible suffering. Many were possessed, went mad and died. But those who escaped possession committed to spending the rest of their lives searching the world for a cure. Eventually they succeeded. They developed a deep understanding of the ways of all kinds of magic and discovered the Firestone. But in the process they found something else: a new way of life, and their wanderings became an eternal quest for knowledge. Not for the power it could give them but because it could protect them from evil and enable them to help others.

'Long before our time, the Kingdom of Alcazar extended the hand of friendship to these wandering people. We provided them with shelter from the most terrible desert storm anyone had ever seen. In return for that kindness they remained as guests and shared much of their knowledge of the world and its many secrets. It was they who taught us what we know of the evil magic and gave us one of their precious Firestones. Eventually, they left to continue their quest for wisdom but, on a number of occasions since, they returned to share the fruits of that quest and to strengthen the bonds of friendship between our two peoples. It is my dearest wish that one day they will return to Alcazar before my days are over, but I fear that may never happen. From time to time travellers passing through Endora's Pool speak of rumours of them or even encounters, but the fact is we haven't seen them for many years. They could be anywhere in the world and may never return to Alcazar.'

'When will you be meeting with the Council of the Wise?' Prince Omar asked.

'The council will convene in two days' time,' Lord Zubin replied, 'and we expect to be putting our proposals to the two kings by the end of the week.'

'Does that mean that the King's coming to Alcazar?' Sir Alfred asked, turning to Lord Balthazar.

'And the Queen,' Lord Balthazar replied. 'They set off the moment your father, Lord Lupus, had been sworn in as Protector of the Realm and moved into the Golden Castle. They should be arriving tomorrow morning.'

'We've planned two days of rejoicing to mark the return of Princess Fleur,' Lord Zubin added, 'and after that we'll all get down to business.'

The next morning, as the sun shone warmly on the Kingdom of Alcazar, Princess Hannah collected Fleur and told her there was a huge surprise waiting outside. She led her out of the Silver Palace and onto the marble steps which led down to the enormous courtyard. All the dignitaries of Alcazar were gathered: the King and Queen, Prince Omar, Princess Leila, Lord Zubin, and the lords and ladies of the Council of the Wise, together with their guests: Lord Balthazar and the knights, Sir Alfred and Sir Luca.

Something special was happening. The courtyard was flanked on all sides by three rows of cavalry: the Silver Riders of Alcazar in their magnificent white ceremonial robes, silver breast plates and sky-blue sashes. And in front of them a line of footmen with long silver horns gleaming in the sun. All round the walls, the flags of both Alcazar and the Golden Kingdom fluttered side by side in the breeze, while thousands of people looked down from their windows and balconies, waving and cheering.

'What on earth's happening?' Fleur asked.

'Look,' Princess Leila replied, pointing into the sky, 'it's the magic carpet.'

And as Fleur watched its approach she could see that it too was decked from bow to stern with the golden flags of home and the sky-blue flags of Alcazar. As it reached the ground the horns sounded triumphantly and the Silver Riders flashed their scimitars to the sky in salute. The captain of the carpeteers handed his passengers down and Fleur could see who they were. It was her mother and father, the King and Queen of the Golden Kingdom. With a little squeal of excitement she pulled her hand free from Princess Hannah's and bounded down the steps as fast as she could, tears of joy streaming down her cheeks. As soon as the King and Queen saw her they threw protocol and royal dignity to the wind and sprinted across the courtyard towards her. And as they swept her into their arms a huge cheer reverberated around the courtyard and the whole of Alcazar joined in the tears of joy.

'There's someone else who wants to give you a big hug,' the Queen said at last, with a huge smile on her face. 'Look who's here.'

To Fleur's delight, it was Hazel, and she'd brought Monkey.

For the rest of the day Alcazar enjoyed the biggest celebration it had seen for years. There was marvellous food and magical entertainment, and Lord Zubin was overjoyed to hear Fleur horrifying Hazel with her account of how she'd been grabbed by those beasts at Barnaby's Mill.

'The treatment must be starting to work,' he said to Lord Balthazar with a broad grin.

Not surprisingly, all this excitement proved a little too much for Fleur and by early evening she gave into fatigue once more. Hazel carried her to bed and tucked Monkey in beside her. Instinctively Fleur took him into her arms and held him tight, as she'd done so many times before. Hazel gave her a loving kiss on the forehead, turned down the bedside lamps and opened the door to leave. But as she did something very strange happened. Monkey suddenly winked at her. The biggest wink she'd ever seen. Hazel nearly jumped out of her skin. She'd always been a sensible girl and didn't believe in magical monkeys for one moment.

She told herself that it couldn't really have happened. It must have been a trick of the light or an illusion brought on by tiredness after her long journey across the desert? What's more, she'd known Monkey for years and he'd never once done anything like that before. But her heart told her something rather different. Somehow that ancient, threadbare monkey with half a tail was telling her there was no longer any need to worry about Princess Fleur. This terrible adventure was over and from now on everything was going to be fine, just as it had been before that terrible day at Barnaby's Mill.